# SHOOT OUT

The instant Surratt's hand moved, Preacher knew the gun fighter was staring at his coat. Preacher also reckoned that Surratt was too professional to expect a draw from the hip. Preacher didn't disappoint his opponent. He drew the custom .44-.40 from his vest holster and shot Kyle Surratt right between the eyes. The force of the blow was just enough to shift Surratt's pistol slightly off target. The barrel was also jerked upward and the shot missed clean.

Preacher holstered his gun just as Indian Charlie and the stage driver, Tim Flannery, emerged.

"That was the fastest pull I've ever see'd *anybody* make," Flannery said.

# Also in the PREACHER'S LAW Series by Dean McElwain:

WIDOW MAKER

# PREACHER'S LAW #2
# TRAIL OF DEATH

## Dean L. McElwain

LEISURE BOOKS  ∞  NEW YORK CITY

*This book
is dedicated to:
Donny Erickson, Ed Gardner and
Gina Polley McElwain
The 'In-Laws' who saved the 'Outlaws'*

A LEISURE BOOK

Published by

Dorchester Publishing Co., Inc.
6 East 39th Street
New York, NY 10016

Copyright©1987 by Dean McElwain

All rights reserved. No part of this book may be reproduced or transmitted by any form or by any electronic or mechanical means, including photocopying, recording, or by any information storage and retrieval system, without the written permission of the Publisher, except where permitted by law.

Printed in the United States of America

# TRAIL OF DEATH

# 1

The man in the saddle was ass tired and bone weary and Dodge City, Kansas, looked damned inviting. Besides that, Preacher was cold. It was nearing the end of April but it felt more like February. A raw, cutting wind swept across the open country, right out of the north. It was a bitter reminder of the brutal winter just past. The man called Preacher reckoned that the winter of '70 and '71 would be one the old timers jawed about around the pot bellies.

Dodge City, like most of the prairie cowtowns, was more facade than substance. Hastily built frameworks of kindling wood hidden by gaudy, outsized fronts. At least two spots did offer a wayfarer touches of grandeur. They were the Dodge House and Chalk Beeson's Long Branch saloon.

Preacher stabled his big chestnut stallion, Cap'n, and stored his saddle. The rest of his gear stayed with him and he ambled off down Front Street toward the Dodge House. He wasn't concerned about finding quarters. It was too early yet for the big trail herds that came up from Texas, and he was glad. Riding with most of them was usually a gunny or two who just had to try his hand. Preacher was there on business. His business. He was a bounty hunter.

J.D. Preacher had ridden out of Bradburn Hill, Tennessee, as a mere boy. He served as a powder monkey with an artillery outfit and, at 18, joined Colonel John Mosby's Rangers. He proved to be one of Mosby's best.

At war's end, Preacher's life was torn asunder. Carpetbaggers—former members of Quantrill's butchers—burned his family's home, killed his parents and rode off with his sister and his fiance. Armed with the skills he'd acquired during the war, and those passed to him by his pioneer father, Jeremy James David Preacher set himself upon a trail of justice . . . and vengeance.

Befriended by a gambler and gunman, Morgan Lake, Preacher honed his skill with pistols until it was as natural an action to him as breathing. Then, one by one, he sought out and killed those who had wronged him. The last man on the list was his own brother, Zachary.

By March 6, 1869—Preacher's 23rd birthday—he had killed 23 men. Fourteen of them left wives behind, and he had earned the public's attention, and a nickname—the Widow Maker.

He had once pinned on the tin star of a lawman, but it had been only in exchange for information. That job done, he steadfastly refused to assume the role fulltime, but not that he lacked for offers. They came from a widely diverse group of sources—a town council, the Pinkerton Agency, and even the White

# TRAIL OF DEATH

House. Preacher shunned them all and rode, alone, in the shadowy no man's land between the law and the lawless. He lived by his wits, his skills and a philosophy which a young reporter had come to call "Preacher's Law."

He rode into Kansas in early '71 to collect a $1000 bounty at Fort Leavenworth. While there, he found *Wanted* dodgers on a pair of murdering misfits named Brock Sturgis and Mexican Joe Juniper. A young deputy marshal who was trailing them got himself killed down in the badlands, but the word came they were drifting north. The first town they would have to pass through would be Dodge City.

Preacher got a hot bath, a shave, and some badly needed sleep. By evening he was back on the job. He ate a hearty meal at the Dodge House and then found his way to the poker tables at the Long Branch. The men he sought, well heeled with blood money, would find it best spent there—if they were in Dodge City at all.

Chalk Beeson, the stocky, mustachioed saloon owner, had set down some hard rules. Hard at least by frontier standards. Personal arguments were to be settled in the street, and the Long Branch's fairy-belles, as Dodge's saloon ladies were known, were to be treated with respect, payed in advance, plus they got a commission on the drinks. Finally, Beeson maintained one of his own men at every gaming table as an active participant. The house got its share of all winnings that way. He ran honest tables and maintained law and order—mostly as a result of his own skills. They were not to be taken lightly.

"Excuse me sir." Preacher looked up from a just completed hand of poker and found himself looking at a very beautiful woman. "Mr. Beeson would appreciate it if you would join him for a drink . . . in his private quarters."

"And who is Mr. Beeson?"

"He owns the Long Branch," the woman replied, still smiling.

"And you're his *messenger?*"

"I'm Dora Hand. I manage the ladies for Mr. Beeson."

"An' she's a helluva lot more than a messenger," the man next to Preacher said. His tone was agitated and his expression less than friendly.

Preacher considered him for a moment, smiled, nodded and said, "I'll remember."

"Mr. Beeson told me to tell you he keeps a fine stock of *Teton Jack*," Dora said. The revelation caught Preacher by surprise. The excellent liquor was rare, and the only thing Preacher ever drank. Few, *very* few people were aware of that fact.

"Lead the way," Preacher said, standing. Dora did, and soon they were in Chalk Beeson's office. Dora poured them each a drink and Preacher noticed a dozen bottles of *Teton Jack* reposing in Beeson's private stock. Dora then excused herself.

"I'm impressed," Preacher said. He hefted the shot glass and Beeson, wordlessly, followed suit. Beeson nodded toward a chair, and Preacher sat.

"You *are* the Widow Maker. That right?"

"My name is Preacher. That's what I prefer."

Beeson smiled. "Have it your way then. I'll be blunt Preacher, I'd like to hire you."

"I'm not looking for work."

Beeson ignored the first barrier. "We need law here. Dodge is headed for a boom—the biggest yet in Kansas. Way bigger than up north. Abilene, Topeka, even Hays City will all continue, but not from Texas cattle. The herds will be stopping here."

"Without a railhead?"

"The Santa Fe is coming in . . . soon!"

"I'm no lawman."

"Yes you are," Beeson snapped. "You just don't wear a badge."

"You have me at a disadvantage," Preacher said. "You seem to know plenty about me."

With that Beeson opened a desk drawer and removed a stack of newspapers—some were yellowed and dog-eared. Preacher caught a glimpse of a copy of the Bloomfield, Missouri *Vindicator*. The first story of any consequence about him had appeared therein.

"Young fella named Breed, Nathan Breed I believe, seems to have a pretty healthy and dogged interest in you himself, Preacher." He handed the big bounty man a copy of the *Rocky Mountain News*. It was dated March of '69—the issue printed on the very day he'd ridden out of Colorado after burying his past.

Preacher quickly read the story about him. He smiled and looked up. "Breed is right about one thing. I didn't know I'd killed twenty three men."

"I'll pay you five hundred dollars a month, Preacher," Beeson said, tossing the paper aside. Clearly, Preacher thought, this man is all business, all the time. "That's twice what the best lawman in the territory earns. On top of that, you'll have free quarters, free meals, and all the action offered in the Long Branch."

"Why, Beeson?"

"Because you're the best."

Preacher jabbed his index finger onto the top newspaper in the stack. "You believe everything you read?"

"No, but I got a fella workin' for me who saw you

in action. I've spent two years lookin' for you. Left messages with every Sheriff and Marshal in three states and most a' the territories."

"Sorry, Beeson," Preacher replied. "Didn't see any of them, or I would have told you no then."

"I've got some power Preacher, folks respect me. You won't have to answer to any politicians or circuit judges, or anybody else."

"Except you." Beeson nodded. "That's one too many, Beeson. No offense," Preacher said, holding up his hand. "I'm a loner. I like it that way."

"What *will* it take?"

"I'm not for sale Beeson, at any price."

"I don't want *you* Preacher, not in that sense of the word. I want, uh, let me say it different. I *need* your guns."

"I'm flattered Beeson," Preacher said, standing up, "I'm just not interested." Beeson sighed and got to his own feet. He reached down behind his desk and produced a bottle of *Teton Jack*.

"My compliments," Beeson said. "I took you away from your game."

Preacher didn't reach out for the bottle but, instead said, "There is something I'd rather have . . . if you've got it."

"If I've got it Preacher, and if I can *give* it, it's yours. So is the whiskey, please."

"Thanks, I'm grateful."

"What else can I do for you?"

"I'm looking for two men. Brock Sturgis and one they call Mexican Joe Juniper."

"You staying in Dodge?"

"At the Dodge House."

"I'll ask around and get word to you." Now Preacher did extend his hand and Beeson took it, firmly. "Will you just *think* about my offer?"

# TRAIL OF DEATH

Beeson was making a final stab at turning the big bounty man's thinking around. He got a surprising and somewhat humorous reply.

"I'm sure of it, Beeson. Damn near everytime I'm sitting out in the cold or the rain or dogging some bastard's trail and I've run out of *this.*" He indicated the whiskey, then he grinned.

Beeson laughed. "By God, Preacher . . . I hope that's real often."

The two men walked back to the gaming table, shook hands again and, as he started to walk away, Beeson turned. "Call me Chalk from now on, Preacher." Preacher nodded. He also noted the changes in facial expressions around him when Beeson spoke his name.

Preacher folded his last hand about midnight. He'd lost two hundred dollars and at the moment it was really more than he could afford. He'd just ordered a new weapon from Colt's company and replenished his trail supplies. He nodded a good night to his table companions, put on his hat, picked up the whiskey bottle with his left hand, and walked toward the door.

"May I buy you a drink?" Preacher turned and saw Dora Hand. "Please?" He followed her to a table. He felt a warm tingling in his groin as Dora bent forward to take her seat. Her cleavage hinted at a promise Preacher thought the rest of her was capable of keeping. Preacher had often thought that his choice of occupations carried with it man's worst enemy—enforced celibacy.

The drinks were served and the two each took several sips before Dora spoke again. "I'm *not* here at Mr. Beeson's request."

"Don't recall saying you were."

"You didn't, but I don't want you even thinking

it, about either of us."

"You always call him *mister* Beeson?"

"Yes. Publicly anyway."

"You don't look . . . well . . ."

She grinned. "Like gambling hall queen? I am what I am. What I once was doesn't matter. Does it?"

"No."

"Aren't you the same Preacher, in a way?"

"In a way."

"Well, I did have a reason for making my invitation. I'd like to hire you."

*Damn*, Preacher thought, *the potential employers are looking better every minute*.

"Chalk wanted the same thing."

"One day, no badge, three hundred dollars. I've got a stage coach full of girls coming up from Liberal. The man I hired to escort them is trying to extort more money from me. I'd like him to understand that I've no intention of paying it."

"Beeson know?"

"He *knows* but we have an agreement. It doesn't include nursemaiding me, or my girls."

"One day? Liberal's a good hard two day ride, just there."

"You ride out half a day, meet the stage, deliver my message, and see to it the man believes it. Then bring them on back. Day after tomorrow."

"Chalk won't because of your agreement?"

"I didn't ask him. I *did* ask one or two of his men. Frankly, they're afraid of this fellow."

"Who is he?"

"Kyle Surratt."

"I've heard of him."

"He's a deadly man with a gun," Dora said. "That's why I hired him. Still, he knows better than to ride into Dodge, and surely better than to come in here. I got this," she added, "two days ago." Dora slipped a small, folded paper from between her breasts. Preacher took it and read.

> Two hundred dollars a head lady—delivered alive. Dead—fifty. You meet me at Bluff Creek crossing in five days, with the money.
>
> Surratt

Preacher handed the paper back. He picked up the *Teton Jack,* stood up, smiled and said, "I'll take the job, and now I'll say goodnight." Dora watched the man in black depart the Long Branch. She knew he was a man she could soon learn to like . . . a lot.

# 2

Bluff Creek crossing was about twenty miles due south of Dodge City. Indian Charlie Keystone ran the way station—a two room, log and soddy structure with a lean-to for the stage stock. Indian Charlie was a half breed Kiowa, built like a grizzly bear and with a temperament to match. He lived alone, occasionally entertained himself with a squeaky, fiddle rendition of *Sweet Betsy from Pike*, and greeted all comers with a .60 calibre *Kaintuck' Long* as he called his rifle.

Preacher arrived at dawn, and Indian Charlie was there, wide awake, to greet him. He eyed Preacher's black clothing suspiciously, with its *citified* appearance. He spat a wad of chewing cud more than a respectable distance, wiped his chin whiskers and gave Preacher a grunt of approval.

"You want drink or vittles mister?"

"Neither," Preacher said. "I'm waiting for a stage coach full of ladies."

"That a fact. Soldier boy are ya?"
"No."
"Lawman mebbe?"
"No."
"Quiet polecat you be?"
"My daddy used to tell me that if I had nothing to say, the best thing I could do was say it."

Indian Charlie took a long pull from a crockery jug. He gritted half rotting, tobacco stained teeth, swallowed with a choke and then bent his head forward, shook it once and exclaimed, "Goddam that's good."

Preacher grinned. "You know a gent called Surratt?"

Indian Charlie frowned. "I heard tell of him. Meaner'n bronc full of loco weed."

"He'll be coming in with that stage I mentioned. We may have some trouble and I'd like to ask that you get the women inside, the driver too. Keep an eye on them until I can settle accounts with Surratt."

"And if he settles you? He'll figger me for backin' ya."

"Uh huh, I'd say that's a fair guess."

"Well?"

"Kill him," Preacher said, pointing to the long rifle. "Or doesn't that thing work."

"It works. Take the wings off a fly at a hundred yards." Such tales always amused Preacher. He'd heard his share too, but he'd learned it was merely the speaker's way of saying he was good. "Fought Bill Cody once . . . back in sixty. Blew blade off an axe at a hundred yards." The old man dug around in a gunny sack and produced a tintype. He handed it to Preacher. It depicted a man he quickly recognized as William F. Cody, and a much younger looking

Charlie Keystone. It was signed by Cody.

"You get anything out of the match besides this picture," Preacher said.

"Sure did. Brand new repeatin' rifle. Lost it," Charlie said, whisking off his hat and bending down so that Preacher could see the top of his head, "same time I lost this." He pointed and Preacher could see the ugly scar of the scalping knife and the resulting bald spot. "Comanche." Charlie grinned, shifted the chaw in his cheek, spit and said, "I ripped off his balls with my bare hand. Don't b'lieve them that tell you Comanche won't howl."

Indian Charlie's dog set up quite a racket with his barking. Preacher got to his feet, Charlie picked up the long rifle and both men went outside. The stage was coming hard, just ahead of the cloud of dust it was stirring up. "Remember Charlie, women and the driver inside." Charlie nodded. Preacher slipped under the low roof of the lean-to.

Satisfied by the driver's identification, Charlie Keystone herded the women inside. The driver followed but Charlie kept the other man engaged in conversation. He noted the man's interest in the lone horse which was tethered at the hitching rail. Finally, Indian Charlie picked up his long rifle and headed inside.

"Who owns the horse, old man?"

"I do," Preacher said, emerging from the lean-to. Charlie looked at both men and then went inside.

Kyle Surratt was a short, shifty eyed man with his left arm gone at the elbow. A souvenir, so he told it, from *Antietam*. He carried what appeared to be an Allen & Wheelock, side hammer revolver. It was a .31 calibre pistol with a short barrel. He wore it in a battered, leather holster, waist level with the butt protruding toward his right hand. Preacher knew he

# TRAIL OF DEATH

was no second rate gunny.

"Who the hell are you?"

"I'm here from Dodge with a message from Dora Hand."

"*Message*? You'd best be totin' some cash."

"First things first," Preacher responded, coolly. "She instructed me to tell you to go to hell. By the way, Mister Surratt, my name is Preacher." Kyle Surratt blinked. It was his only reaction but it was tell-tale enough. He did it three times, rapidly.

"The fancy Dan gun man. Bounty hunter too as I recollect."

"Ride out Surratt. South. I've got the money you were supposed to get in my pocket."

"I'm gonna kill you gun man."

"Mebbe. Then, old Indian Charlie inside the shack is going to blow your head off with a Kentucky long rifle."

"I heard you wasn't much on talkin'," Surratt said, grinning as he remembered what he'd read. "You just kill 'em an' ride off. That right, Widda Maker?" Surratt's right hand suddenly became a blur. The shot from the old *Allen & Wheelock* whizzed past Preacher's head on the left side, about ear level. Surratt *was* fast, damned fast.

J. D. Preacher once again benefitted however from the edge he always enjoyed. It was enhanced by the fact that he carried two pistols—one in a shoulder holster sewn to the left side of his vest, just below his armpit, the other on his right hip. Surratt had spotted both. He was a professional and most of them *did* spot both. They could never be certain which gun Preacher would use. His speed was the same regardless of his choice.

The instant Surratt's hand moved, Preacher knew the gun fighter was staring at his coat. Preacher also reckoned that Surratt was too professional to expect a draw from the hip. Preacher didn't disappoint his opponent. He drew the custom .44-.40 from his vest holster and shot Kyle Surratt right between the eyes. The force of the blow was just enough to shift Surratt's pistol slightly off target—Preacher's left nipple. The barrel was also jerked upward and the shot missed clean.

Preacher holstered his gun just as Indian Charlie and the stage driver, Tim Flannery, emerged.

"That was the fastest pull I've ever see'd *anybody* make," Flannery said.

Indian Charlie Keystone was more interested in Preacher's accuracy. He knelt over Surratt's body, studied the wound, stood up, removed his hat, scratched his head and said, "Jehosophat!"

"Name's Flannery mister, Tim Flannery an' I'm more'n a little proud to make your acquaintance." He held out a leathery hand. Preacher took it.

"Preacher," was all he said.

"The bounty hunter?" Preacher nodded. Flannery let out a long, low whistle. "I figgered he had you sure. I seen Surratt cut down two men in El Paso one night. Already had the drop on 'im."

Preacher ignored the tale and asked Charlie to get the women. He wanted to get back to Dodge City. He had a job to do and it wasn't getting done. He turned to Flannery, still open mouthed over the confrontation. "Grab his legs, we'll load him up."

"Hold it Preacher," Charlie hollered. He was herding the women outside. There were six and two of them eyed Preacher with looks which would have melted a cannon barrel. "I want you to leave that corpse for me to bury." Preacher frowned. Charlie grinned. "Good for business. He had a name. Died here. Buried here. It make for drinking business while I tell how it happened."

"No matter to me," Preacher said. "And you'll get the burying fee."

Charlie smiled his yellow-toothed grin.

Dora Hand gave Preacher three crisp $100 bank notes. She also offered him a bonus. It grated on him that he couldn't accept it. He reasoned that he couldn't afford another day's delay. Sturgis and Joe Juniper didn't roost too long in any one spot. He definitely wanted to catch them at their next one.

Chalk Beeson told Preacher that the duo had been in Dodge. Someone at the livery overheard them talking about moving on to Abilene. They had an old score to settle with the city marshal.

"I'll be back to collect that bonus," Preacher said to Dora.

"Then I'll make you a better offer next time around." She smiled.

"I hope I'll have sense enough not to ride away from it." Preacher winced.

He was surprised to find Chalk Beeson waiting for him at the livery. Chalk made his final plea to Preacher while the bounty man saddled Cap'n. Preacher listened. He finally backed Cap'n out of the stall and walked the big stallion outside. Then, he turned to the saloon owner.

"Chalk, I like you. I can't say that about too many men. I don't get that close. You're only the second that I'd ever consider, seriously consider, working for."

"Who's the first, damn it? Mebbe I can talk sense to *him*."

Preacher grinned. "I wish I knew where he was, I'd let you give it a try. Jim Hickok."

"Gawdamighty! Wild Bill Hickok?"

21

## Dean McElwain

"We're friends. I did a scouting job for him in '68 down on the Washita."

"You two get together, *ever* again, you got to promise me you'll come to Dodge. Both of you. Why, I put you two on Front Street at the same time and the whole damned town would be like a church social."

Preacher mounted up. "Well if you see him Chalk, tell him I've still got his dispatch case." Chalk Beeson and J.D. Preacher shook hands. Both quietly wondering if they would ever see each other again.

It's a long, lonely trail to follow between Dodge City and Albilene. Up along the Arkansas river to Great Bend and out past Cheyenne Bottoms lake. Preacher stayed south, skirting the town of Salina, rode due east, and cut north at Sand Spring and into Abilene. He'd heard much about the town they called the *Sodom* of the plains. He wasn't disappointed.

# 3

Preacher holed up in the Texas hotel. He needed the rest and he knew better than to ask too many questions about his quarry. Unlike Dodge City in that early May of 1871, there *was* law in Abilene—Bear River Tom Smith, the city marshal. Mostly he kept the peace with ham-sized fists, but if the situation dictated it, he toted two short-barreled shotguns. Just a smidgen above outright lawbreakers, Marshal Tom Smith listed bounty men as his most unfavorite types.

Preacher learned that the Marshal was delivering a prisoner to the sheriff in Salina. He'd be gone two or three days and there was no deputy. Preacher also recognized the nature of the men he was trailing. While both were skilled gunmen, either would backshoot a man with no remorse or hesitation.

On the morning of his third day in Abilene, he developed a serious case of cabin fever. An inquiry at the front desk about the source of local action led him directly to the Alamo saloon. If Abilene was nothing else, it was damned grateful to Texans and the herds of cattle they drove north to the railroad. On the cowtown's main street alone, a visitor could stay at the Texas Hotel, gamble in the El Paso bar, the Alamo saloon or Houston's Emporium. The latter also furnished up an abundance of sporting ladies.

Five men merely nodded up when Preacher inquired about joining their game. One, obviously a professional, informed Preacher of the $100 minimum opening.

He pulled his hand only far enough apart to identify the cards. Two Kings, a three, a seven and a five. The opening bet was two hundred. Preacher kicked in fifty dollars—the minimum table bet. One man folded.

"Cards?" the professional queried Preacher.

"Two." He saw the gambler's eyes shift to the man next to Preacher. Preacher was certain that both he and the gambler knew what the man was holding. Three of a kind. Cards dealt, the betting resumed. Preacher never touched his three card *keep* or the two he'd been dealt. He was bluffing on three of a kind and he intended to ride it out. The betting and raising rounded the table twice, thinning the participants to three.

"I'll have to raise the last bet by another two hundred," the professional said. Preacher was quick to oblige. The man next to him, the only player other than the professional who was still in, hedged. He studied his hand with an intensity which seemed to portray the idea that the cards would, somehow, change their spots if he stared hard enough. Finally, he called the bet.

The professional had drawn only one card.

# TRAIL OF DEATH

Preacher was confident he'd been drawing to a straight. In fact, the professional displayed three tens.

"Perhaps now sir," the professional said, "you'll have to see if you drew that fourth match." He was smiling. Preacher had convinced *him* that he was already holding three. Preacher reached out and flipped both cards over. A King and a five.

"Seems I beat my own luck," Preacher said. He'd tossed in the seven and the three. He was now holding a full house, Kings and fives! The man next to him groaned when he exposed the last of his cards. The professional shrugged.

"Well played sir, very well played indeed." Preacher raked in the pot. "If you gentlemen will excuse me, I'll go and relieve myself." The professional got up and disappeared toward the rear of the saloon. The out-houses were sequestered at the back of the Alamo, just outside the rear door. Two other men also left the table, one to join the gambler. The other sauntered to the bar.

"Oh Mother of God!" Preacher had just shifted positions in his chair. He looked up. The one man remaining at the table, seated almost opposite Preacher's chair, was staring toward the rear of the saloon. His eyes were big, round, and full of fear. A shot rang out.

Preacher was already moving to his left and down. That fact aside, the bullet ripped through Preacher's hat, carrying it into the face of the man who'd shouted. The bullet, of course, had preceded the hat. The man was dead.

Preacher drew his hip pistol on the way down, rolled completely over once and came up in a crouch. A second shot had already splintered the back of the chair in which he was sitting. Preacher fired at the gambler, killing him with a shot through the heart. Preacher got to his feet. The crowd, by no means unaccustomed to gunplay, quickly resumed its previous activities. Only a tall, well dressed man who'd been standing at the bar approached Preacher.

"Name was Thelonius Jones," the well dressed man said. He extended his hand, "Mine is Ben Thompson, late of El Paso, Texas. I watched Jones lose about $8000 over the last day or so." Thompson smiled. "You must have cleaned him out."

Preacher, his gun still in his hand, didn't acknowledge Thompson's comments or even his presence. Instead, he turned slowly around, eyeing the other patrons, looking for any sign of another possible assassin. Half satisfied that the gambler had acted alone, Preacher moved to the bar, holstered his gun and stood, back to the bar with his elbows resting on its edge.

"Glad to make your acquaintance," he said, looking at Thompson. He still didn't return the amenity of shaking hands.

"You're a cautious man sir." Thompson gestured toward Jones' body. "Of course if that kind of thing happens often, I can understand why. May I buy you a drink?"

Preacher considered Thompson. He was a tall, stately looking man, attired in a fine broadcloth suit, checkered vest, string tie and all topped with a silk plug hat. He was no dude, Preacher concluded. He wore a waist holster, tipped forward on his left side. In it reposed a short barrel Remington .44, butt first.

"Why?" Preacher finally asked.

"I'm looking for a partner. A man who can gamble, handle himself, and enjoys the finer things of life. I noticed for instance," Thompson continued, smiling, "that you avoid the house whiskey and tote your own. Special mix?"

"*Teton Jack,*" Preacher said. "Hard to come by out here."

"Wouldn't be in our place," Preacher looked into Thompson's face. The man was smiling. Preacher was somewhat moved by the man's presumptuous attitude. "Barkeep, do you have *Teton Jack?*" The barkeep shook his head. Thompson shrugged. "Nothing then." He turned back to Preacher. "Perhaps we can retire to my room and discuss some business . . . if you're interested."

"I'm not, Thompson," Preacher replied. "I'm no gambler by profession and I'm not much on partners, no offense."

"None taken, mister." Thompson stopped, smiled and made Preacher realize that he'd never told Thompson his name.

"No mister, just Preacher."

"Ah yes, the bounty man. You've acquired some measure of renown even down my way . . . Texas." Thompson grinned and Preacher noted a swell of pride in the man's chest and in the tone he applied to the name Texas. "As you know, Texans are not easily impressed."

"No Thompson, I can't say as I did know it. I don't recall ever having tried to impress one." Thompson's facial muscles tensed for a moment. He stared and then slowly began to smile. Ultimately, he was laughing and he finally shook his head.

"Preacher, you're a hell of a man. I like you. If you ever change your mind, look me up. I'll be easy to find."

The exchange was interrupted by a short, balding man who introduced himself as Eli Maphis. "I was told what happened and that you, sir, were the intended victim." He was looking up at Preacher.

"It appeared I was."

"I'm not a lawman sir, but I've agreed to assist the city marshal in his absence. I'm certain that the events which occured did so as I've heard, but the marshal's rule requires that I ask for your gun."

"Then," Preacher replied in an icy tone, "you've followed the rule. You've asked." Thompson grinned. Maphis swallowed.

"I—I don't think you understand me sir."

"I understand. Now *you* understand. My gun stays with me. I was told the marshal will be back in a day or two. I'll be around. Tell him to come see me if he has any questions. I'll either be here or in my room at the hotel."

"He won't like this," Maphis said, trying to convey an ominous tone.

"I didn't like what happened to me either," Preacher said. He straightened. "Maybe the marshal should have you transferring prisoners and he should stay in town and do his job." Preacher turned to Thompson. "I'm grateful for your offer Thompson. Good luck to you." He turned to Maphis. "Good night," he said.

The door to Preacher's room slammed into the corner of the heavy chiffoneir. Part of the door frame was splintered and one of the panels was smashed, the result of a heavy boot which had kicked it in. Preacher was clearly caught defenseless. The light from the corridor's gas lamps silhouetted a man's figure standing where the door had been. The man held a shotgun.

Preacher's hand had found the pistol which he always kept under his pillow. Beneath the blanket

# TRAIL OF DEATH

now, its barrel was leveled at the man's chest. Still, Preacher knew, at best, he was in a fight which could only end in a tie.

"You're under arrest," the man said. Preacher frowned as the voice stirred something inside him. "Unless," the voice continued, "you've got a pistol on me." The shotgun came down, the man leaned it against the chiffoneir. He picked up the lamp, fished for a match, lit the lamp, turned around and held the lamp in front of him.

"Jeezus Christ," Preacher bellowed. "I could have shot you."

"Yeah, I got to figurin' that." Then, Jim Hickok broke into a hearty laugh.

As tired as he'd been, the surprise visit from Hickok had sharpened Preacher's wits. It also taught him another life and death lesson.

"If I'd been a friend o' that gambler's, the buryin' man would have another double in the mornin'. Ought to prop a chair in front o' the door an' run a string across in front o' the window. I usually tie it to the wash pitcher. Anybody comin' in will pull it onto the floor."

"Yeah," Preacher said, disgustedly. "I acted like a damned greenhorn."

"Not enough—you'da killed me."

As they ate breakfast at barely past four o'clock, Hickok talked of his recent past. Abilene's marshal, Bear River Smith, had been gunned down by a homesteader in the fall of '70—backshot. Abilene was too wild a town to be with no law at all, but finding a replacement, indeed, finding *any* man who would tackle the job, had proven difficult. Though there were many who were still reluctant, the town council finally agreed to hire Hickok. He had assumed the job only the month before.

"Well Preacher man, what the hell brings you to Abilene?" Hickok grinned. "Sure not just to gun down some tin horn."

"Had to return your dispatch case." Hickok laughed. "Truth is, I'm out for bounty. Brock Sturgis and Mexican Joe Juniper."

"Heard o' Sturgis. Other name don't seem familiar." Hickok leaned back in his chair and rubbed his nose. He looked serious. "Don't think they're here but if they are, I need to know it my friend." Preacher knew what Hickok inferred.

"You'll know, Jim."

"Fair enough." Hickok poured more coffee for both men and then offered Preacher a Cheroot. Preacher declined. "I could use a deputy."

"I'm not your man, Jim."

"I already owe ya one for that scoutin' job down on the Washita. I didn't forget." Hickok leaned forward, resting his elbows on the table and interlocking his fingers. "This would square us. I got three men comin' in . . . gunnin' for me. I got dodgers on ever' damn one of 'em. Just took their kid brother over to Salina. They're worth ten thousand all totalled. Local money, ever' penny. It's yours Preacher man."

"If I put on a badge?"

Hickok nodded. "Abilene cattle buyers put it up. This outfit's been rustlin'. Cost the buyers fifty thousand last year. Prices are up. Be half that much again this year. They're gettin' off cheap."

"And what the hell do *you* get out of it, Jim?"

"The credit." Preacher frowned. He'd heard plenty of stories about Jim Hickok's ego, and the eastern press had already made *Wild Bill* a legend. Preacher knew the man or so he thought.

"What the hell do you need that for? There's not a

marshal's job, or scouting job you couldn't get right now, just by asking." Hickok smiled. It was a pathetic smile. He leaned back and tugged at his right ear.

"Only damn thing I *do* want I can't seem to pull together. Like to get in on somethin' worthwhile. A Texas herd mebbe, or some railroad stock or some land. Somethin' that's mine, somethin' besides a badge or a deck o' cards or a pistol. Trouble is, nobody'll stake me."

"But if you stop this rustling and the buyers know it. . . ." Hickok was already nodding. "Goddamn you, Jim. You're the only son-of-a-bitch that can talk me into something I don't want to do."

Hickok smiled a wry smile. "Is that a yes?"

"Go to hell," Preacher said. Hickok laughed.

# 4

The rustlers about whom Hickok had related his tale were the Bent brothers. The youngest, Stace, couldn't hold his liquor, his mouth, or his gun. It had cost him his freedom. The others were another matter. They were Kane, Pete and Bo—all experienced trail hands, and more than ready with both handguns and rifles.

They had wintered in New Orleans, living easy and high off their ill-gotten funds from the previous year. Pickings were increasing and by 1871, herds from Texas had doubled in size and in numbers. The railheads in Kansas were now scattered from Abilene down through Ellsworth and Hays City, and soon there would be even more. Most of the towns were wide open.

While scores of men were attracted to the money represented by the herds, and most didn't care how they got it, damned few were interested in protecting the windfall. Even fewer were really qualified to do it. Men like Bear River Smith knew the risks they took. He lived with the daily threat of what finally happened to him. He and Hickok and a handful of others took the risks for anywhere from fifty to a hundred and fifty dollars a month. The same money was available by rustling three or four cows. Half a dozen men could rustle a hundred head almost undisturbed.

The big herds began to arrive in the Kansas cowtowns in mid June, and the drives continued through July. The Bent brothers rode into Abilene on the 22nd day of May and took up residence in Houston's Emporium.

Kane Bent quickly took a shine to the casino manager, a ravishing, raven haired Creole girl named Lurilene Breaux. Kane had misinterpreted Lurilene's zealous welcome. She had assumed them to be the point riders for one of the big cattle outfits, but by the time she had recognized her mistake, it was too late.

The Bent boys gambled and drank their two days in town away. Once or twice when someone attempted to interfere with Kane's domination of Lurilene's time, they were met with frightening threats. Still, the Bent boys seemed in no hurry to outright break the law and force a confrontation with the town's infamous marshals. Neither had Kane attempted to force his unwanted affection on the hapless casino manager—not, at least, until the early evening of the third day.

"Where you tryin' to git to girl," Kane said, his arm tightening around Lurilene's hips.

"I've got to count the day's receipts," she said, smiling and trying to remain nonchalant.

Kane Bent grinned, blew cheeks full of blue-gray smoke into her face and said, "Think we'll do that job together this evenin'. Whatta *you* think?"

"I . . . I guess it would be alright but, I've got to do it soon. You know, before the evening customers start coming."

"Sure you do," Kane said, "sure. An' we will. Soon as I finish takin' this gent's money." Kane grinned across the table at a rotund drummer of men's shirts. He'd attempted to leave a game at which he'd been losing for most of the afternoon but Kane wouldn't let him. When the drummer ran out of money, Kane went to work on the drummer's stock of shirts. Quite an expensive and sizeable selection which the drummer had made the mistake of talking about early on.

"I've only a . . . a few good shirts left," the man said. Kane Bent turned Lurilene loose and leaned forward, menacingly. "Then we'll play some cards for the Goddam bad shirts. Won't we, drummer?" The man nodded, weakly.

Lurilene was seething inside. She had managed to slip a dozen or more messages out of the Emporium to the marshal, but Hickok had not made an appearance. The Emporium was open all night but Hickok had even avoided his usual stop when he made his nightly rounds. Lurilene herself had been unable to slip away, because Kane Bent had forced her to stay in her office when she was not with him.

The other Bent boys had also remained in the Emporium. Either in the company of one of the girls, or at one of the many gambling tables. Kane forbid them to separate. The few men at the Emporium who had shown even mild resistance to the Bent's activities had been frightened off. Others concluded that if Wild Bill Hickok was too scared to show up, they had no business interfering.

Preacher, having heard the stories and the word

on the streets of Abilene, finally ran out of patience. He knew Hickok's reputation for doing things his own way but this seemed too far afield.

Hickok arrived back at his office about five o'clock in the afternoon. Preacher was waiting for him. "Jim, what do you intend to do about the Bent boys, and when?" The tone of the inquiry was more demanding than Hickok liked. He clenched his teeth and said nothing. He removed his hat, poured himself a shot of whiskey, sat down at his desk, downed the shot and then looked up.

"Haven't heard any complaints from the citizen's council."

"The citizen's council isn't holed up in the Emporium."

"Anxious to collect that ten thousand are you?" Now it was Preacher who bristled. Mostly, he didn't understand the rather sudden change in his old friend's attitude.

"I'm more anxious to take off this badge. I don't relish being a walking target."

"When I'm ready to move on the Bents, Preacher man, you'll be the first to know." Hickok reached for a stack of papers and began to sort through them. Preacher wasn't used to being put off. Not even from the likes of James Butler Hickok.

"That's not good enough," Preacher said.

"Don't push it," Hickok snapped. He looked up when the badge bounced on the desk top. "Didn't figure you for a quittin' man."

"Then that's *two* mistakes you've made lately," Preacher replied. He walked to the door and turned back. "In your job that's not healthy."

Hickok ignored both comments and said, "I can't stop you from quittin', but I won't tolerate bounty huntin' in Abilene. You got plans to go after the

Bent boys, forget 'em . . . unless they ride out."

"I came looking for Brock Sturgis and Joe Juniper. They're not here—haven't been as far as I can find out. I got no reason to stay." Preacher walked out but he felt suddenly empty inside. He was angry and he didn't like what Jim Hickok had done to him. He'd conjured up old feelings. Feelings Preacher had put behind him when he rode out of Colorado after gunning his brother.

He returned to his hotel and ordered dinner. He found himself just picking at the food. He was restless, so he walked to the livery and checked on Cap'n, then headed back toward the Alamo saloon. Maybe some poker would help. Suddenly, Preacher felt rebellious, angry at a breach in a friendship which he didn't understand. He paused at the corner and looked toward the Emporium. "Damn you Jim," he muttered. He turned on his heel and headed toward the saloon and casino.

He pondered the possible results of what he was planning to do. He was almost as well known in Abilene as was Hickok. When he'd accepted the deputy appointment, the word got out quickly. He too, had avoided the Emporium and the Bent boys at Hickok's order. Now, badge or no badge, he was walking into trouble. Even if he survived it, he'd have Hickok's wrath to face, and maybe the marshal's guns as well.

Preacher drew parallel with the bat wing doors of Houston's Emporium casino and paused. Had he been too hasty with his friend? Jim Hickok was not an impetuous man. He *must* have some plan. Still, why keep it from a deputy? Particularly a deputy who was, supposedly, an old friend.

Preacher removed his black, shallow crowned hat and smoothed his wavy hair. He replaced his hat, shined the toes of his boots on the backside of his pants, adjusted his string tie, smoothed his vest and started to reach for the door.

"Far enough, Preacher man." Preacher whirled. Jim Hickok emerged from the shadows of a doorway across the street. "I warned you about bounty huntin' in Abilene. Also had you figured for ignorin' me, in spite o' your word."

"Jim, what the hell . . ."

"I'll have your guns bounty hunter, right now!" Preacher heard the doors behind him. Someone walked out then stopped, dead in their tracks. A moment later, the doors opened again and whoever had exited now made a fast re-entry. Preacher could hear the voices inside. The word was spreading that Marshal Hickok was arresting his own deputy, a bounty hunter and notorious gunman. It would be the showdown of the century, Wild Bill Hickok and J.D. Preacher, the Widow Maker.

"You know better Jim. I won't give you my guns."

"Then use 'em."

"You know better than that too," Preacher said. He turned completely around, putting his back to the famed lawman. Then, he reached up, pushed both the bat wing doors open and stepped inside the saloon. He was half way to the bar when a man appeared from behind some curtains at the rear of the saloon.

"She run out," he shouted, "I was tryin' to see what was happening' in the street, Kane . . . an' she run out the back. I . . . I'm sorry." Preacher stopped and looked to his left. A tall man shoved a chair back from a table. He was glowering at the young man who'd come from behind the curtains. Preacher quickly took in the situation. The distraction of

Hickok's confrontation outside had finally given Lurilene Breaux a moment to escape.

The bat wings opened. Jim Hickok's booming voice bellowed a command. "I'm down on you Bent boys, give it up." The young man whipped both hands towards his hips. Jim Hickok killed him. Preacher caught the slightest movement to his left and slightly above him. Pete Bent was clad only in his longjohns. He had a shotgun in his hands. Preacher's shot struck the man just below his left ribs and ripped upwards through his body at an angle. It tore up enough inside to finish him.

Kane Bent was a little faster than his reputation implied. He'd cleared leather, whirled back to his right and fired at Hickok even before the marshal's shot had killed young Bo. It was still too late and both Hickok's shot and Preacher's struck the man almost simultaneously. The combined force took him clear off his feet and his body crashed into three or four chairs, two tables and finally banged to the floor.

The blue-gray gunsmoke hung in the air as if tethered to the invisible tension. Both Hickok and Preacher scanned the faces. The women were mostly crouched down. Many of the men had not moved that fast. They stood, open mouthed, in obvious awe of a display of gunplay which defied description.

Ever so slowly, life ebbed into the Emporium once again. It began with Marshal Hickok's own movements. He stuck his pistols back in the red sash around his waist and moved toward Kane Bent's body. Preacher headed up the stairs to make certain that Pete was harmless. There was no need for either of them the check Bo. The Bent brothers were done rustling, or anything else.

"Get back to your business," Hickok shouted,

# TRAIL OF DEATH

"show's over." Lurilene Breaux walked through the front door and Preacher got his first look. It proved not to be his last.

"Jim," Preacher said, "you scare the hell out of me."

"Sorry friend, but we didn't dare move on them boys as long as Luri was in there. I'd planted a half a dozen rumors 'bout some things over the last day or two but they didn't do no good. Figured a showdown between us just might."

"Ever occur to you that I might have been mad enough to pull on you since you didn't bother to let me in on it?"

Hickok cocked his head in thought. "Yeah," he finally said, "I recollect that it did. Once."

"And?"

"And what?"

"And if I had pulled on you damn it, then what?"

"Guess I'da had to shoot you, Preacher man." Hickok half smiled. "Or you would'a shot me. Didn't make no differ'nce. Wasn't you or me I was doin' it for. Long as Luri got out. I figured one or the other of us would have got the Bent boys."

"Jeezus Jim, why in hell didn't you tell me?"

"I figure you for a helluva lot better man with a gun than you are as an actor. I wanted it real." Hickok grinned. "That what scared you?"

"Hell, no," Preacher shouted. "It's that I'm so Goddam predictible and you *knew* it."

Hickok nodded and looked up. "Yeah, I'd say that's worth changin'. In your business, an' mine, man oughtn't to break too many rules or acquire too many bad habits. It's downright unhealthy."

"Besides that," Preacher said, walking to the door, "you got that damned badge back and cost me the bounty. I was supposed to be working for you."

Hickok grinned again. "Look in your left side coat pocket." Preacher reached in, felt something cold, withdrew it and found himself staring down at a tin star. "Slipped it in there a couple o' days back, just in case."

"Predictible," Preacher mumbled, "too damn predictible." In fact, the tall, cool-headed Tennessean with the lightening gun hand had learned another lesson from the Prince of Pistoleers. It was one he'd never forget.

Preacher was shirtless when the knock came at the door of his room. He slipped the pistol out of his vest holster, leveled it at the door and said, "Who is it?"

"Lurilene Breaux." Preacher put the pistol away, picked up his shirt and slipped it on, and then walked to the door. He continued buttoning it after he opened the door. Lurilene walked in, glanced around and then looked up at Preacher. "I brought you a couple of things. Marshal Hickok told me something of what you prefer." She handed Preacher a small, cloth bag. He pushed the door shut, took the bag and then pointed to an overstuffed chair in the room's corner.

"Please, sit down Miss Breaux."

"Call me Luri. The marshal told me you preferred to be called Preacher." Preacher nodded. He finished buttoning his shirt and then tucked it in, turning his back while he buttoned his fly. He opened the little bag. It was a bottle of *Teton Jack*.

"Care for a drink?" Preacher asked.

"A small one, please." He poured them each one.

"Glad you're out of your tight," he said. She looked puzzled. "The spot you were in, with the Bent boys," Preacher continued.

She nodded. "A *tight?*"

He smiled. "That's what some would call it. Tight place."

"It was that. Thank you for getting me out." They gestured to each other with the glasses and both drank. Preacher sat down on the edge of the bed.

"I don't mean to seem . . . greedy," Preacher said, "but you said you brought me a couple of things. Jim send along a message?"

"No." Lurilene Breaux stood up, walked to where she could position herself in front of Preacher and then began to unbutton her dress. She smiled. "The other thing was me."

Lurilene Breaux's Creole heritage extended to every part of her body. Her skin was an almond hue with a texture like silk. Her neck was long and tapered and she was perfectly proportioned for her five and a half feet of height. Her breasts were firm, their tips jutting upwards slightly and appearing perpetually hard.

She slipped from the last of her clothing and made no effort at hiding the promises she had made. The dark, velvety patch between her thighs caught shafts of light from the oil lamp and glistened invitingly. She moved within Preacher's reach, bent forward and kissed him. Then she straightened up and pressed his head against the flat, firm surface of her abdomen.

Preacher kissed her and she threaded her fingers through his hair. He reached up and touched and stroked her breasts while she moaned softly, caught her breath in a sudden gasp and then pulled free of him positioning herself on the bed.

Preacher moved up next to her. They kissed and touched, and then he stripped. She pulled the covers back and Preacher's mind flashed to the face of Rosamond Langehorne. It was a gesture she might have made ... when they wed ... after the war ... before . . . Preacher shoved the pain and the memories away. Rosamonde was dead.

Lurilene Breaux was no whore. At least she was not in the mind of J.D. Preacher. Whores didn't pull bedcovers back. They didn't lay beside a man and kiss his neck, eyelids, nose and his mouth.

Preacher responded to Lurilene and felt a cleanliness he'd almost forgotten. There was meaning to this act, something beyond wild, unabashed passion. There was a man, a woman, combined feelings and a quiet respect for the other's needs, desires and limits.

When Preacher and Luri Breaux finally found one another, they melded their bodies into a single entity. They sought not animal release but the epitomy of human relationship. They reached the pinnacle together, at once blending long dormant desires which they had chosen to keep for someone special.

"Thank you," Luri whispered. "You are wonderful."

"You owed me nothing," Preacher replied.

She kissed him, lightly. "Yes I did. What I owed was in the cloth bag." He kissed Luri and she stayed the night. They shared one another as the sun marked a new day—but this time, they did not speak of it.

# 5

Preacher collected his bounty money on the Bent boys on the 17th of June. It came with the arrival of the first two big herds from Texas. It was late in the afternoon and Preacher opted to spend one more night in Abilene.

He had dinner with Jim Hickok who then had to ride south to meet with two more buyers. Preacher promised to remain in town until Hickok's return the next morning, when they would have a parting drink. Just after seven, Preacher found himself at a poker table in the Alamo saloon. It was a seven man table with six players. '

"Mind if I fill that last seat?" Preacher, now following his friend's good advice and keeping his back always to a wall, thought he recognized the voice. He looked up, and it was big Ben Thompson.

"Sit," Preacher said, gesturing. He glanced around the table for reaction. Thompson, unlike their first meeting, looked somewhat down on his luck. "I know this gent," Preacher said. "He's a fair man." The others nodded.

In fact, Ben Thompson had gone back to Texas and lost his whole bankroll in a crooked cattle deal. One day, he'd sworn, he'd get revenge. He rode back to Abilene, arriving with barely the price of one night's lodging and a meal. Preacher had noticed that Thompson was minus his pistol. He'd sold it to grubstake his game.

The evening's play developed along rather typical lines. Three of the seven chairs lost their original occupants to others. Pots seemed equally divided and of mediocre worth. Outside, a thunderstorm had blown up. It was, in Kansas jargon, a frog strangler.

About eleven o'clock, one of the original players folded his hand and spoke his good nights. A finely attired gent of sizeable proportions approached the table.

"I'll take a few hands, if there are no objections." None were voiced. "I'll buy a round of drinks by way of introduction. My name is Phil Coe." After the introductions were done and the drinks served, Coe produced an enviable stack of bills. He also inherited the deal.

"Stud. Five card." The first card went face down. Four would then be dealt face up with a round of betting on each. The final bet would be made on the hole card. It was a game of professionals where bluffing was as integral as the cards themselves. It was a no limit game.

Coe was seated opposite Preacher but next to Ben Thompson. Thompson was an inch or two taller than Coe but the latter made up for it in width. Still, Preacher had reckoned that Phil Coe was not a soft, fat man. He'd also detected the tell-tale bulge of a pocket pistol.

# TRAIL OF DEATH

There had been generous raises but by the end of the fourth round, only three men remained active. Phil Coe, big Ben Thompson and J.D. Preacher. Preacher was showing a pair of sevens and a deuce. Thompson grinned behind a nine, a ten and a jack of hearts. Phil Coe showed a pair of eights and a four.

"You bet, Preacher."

"A hundred."

Ben Thompson didn't bat an eye. "And a hundred more," he said. Preacher guessed that Thompson was down to his last two or three hundred dollars. He'd done exceedingly well considering he started with a stake of $250.

Preacher caught just a fleeting wrinkle in Phil Coe's brow. Nonetheless, Coe covered the bet and called. "One more gents," he said. He flipped a card over and dropped it in front of Preacher. "A seven." The fleeting wrinkle was now a frown. Preacher was showing three of a kind. Coe forced a smile. He flipped a card in front of Ben Thompson. "You gents make it tough on a fellow." Thompson's eyes sparkled when he saw the eight of hearts drop. Coe dealt himself another four. "Two pair," he said, grinning again. "Preacher?"

The lanky Tennessean was showing everything he had—three sevens. He considered a bluff but one man, Thompson, could have a winner all the way, and wouldn't buy the bluff if his own hole card was the seven of hearts.

"I'll have to fold." Preacher had learned his poker very well over the years since he'd met Morgan Lake on the Mississippi.

Neither Coe or Thompson would be bluffed, not this far into the game. If Preacher bet less than he had been betting, or if he checked, he was simply exposing his hand. A hand he didn't have. Besides, he could drive Thompson out of the game and he had a hunch that the Texas gambler might be holding what he needed.

"Two hundred," Ben said. He was left with a single bill. A fifty. Phil Coe didn't look at Ben Thompson's hand. Instead, he glanced at the lonely fifty dollar bill. He grinned.

"And two hundred more." Preacher was ready to back Thompson. It wasn't his way. Certainly it wasn't a habit. Somehow, he liked this big, gentlemanly Texan. Preacher, and Phil Coe, were in for a surprise. Ben Thompson reached into his vest pocket. He'd been sand-bagging.

"You're called Mister Coe." The blood drained from Phil Coe's face. The pot was well over $2,000. Coe had planned to steal it by simply pushing Thompson out of the game. Still, he was cool headed. After all, he was showing two pair. A hole card matching either pair and he'd have a respectable full house.

"Clever, Mister Thompson," Coe said. "Very clever, but I don't really believe you have that straight flush." Preacher thought he sensed trouble.

"I believe the gentleman called you, Mister Coe."

"Oh yes, no doubt about that," Ben Thompson said, "but I've no quarrel with Mister Coe's opinion. If he's ready to back it."

Coe frowned. "Back it? Sir, it's obvious I can back *my* bet, and I've been called."

"A side bet then. Talk has it that you plan to open a saloon in Abilene. That, sir, is also my ambition. Unfortunately, I am without the necessary funds at present."

"What are you getting at," Coe asked.

"Simple enough. I'm a good house man. I'll wager a year's service to you in your saloon, room and board only, against a one third interest if I win."

"Done," Coe said, without a moment's hesitation. He flipped over his hole card. It was a four! "Full house, Mister Thompson." Ben Thompson's eyes went from Coe's card to Preacher's face.

"You made a wise choice, bounty man. I wouldn't have bought that fourth seven." He flipped his card. The hand almost leaped out and struck big Phil Coe in the face. 7, 8, 9, 10, and jack of hearts!

The sky was a dirty gray but the rain had stopped. What had fallen turned Abilene's streets into seas of mud. The situation was compounded with the passage of many smaller herds of cattle directly through town headed for the pens to the southeast. Preacher watched the procession for more than an hour from the city marshal's office. Jim Hickok finally returned.

"Hate to see you ride out again, Preacher man. Life's too short and good friends too few to part trails too often."

"Well, if you quit carrying a badge and I quit collecting wanted posters, maybe we can figure something else out. We'll cross trails again."

"I hope so," Hickok said. "Where you headed?"
"North."
"Any particular reason?"

"Men like Sturgis and Juniper usually follow the easy pickings. This time of the year that'll be north. They won't try to fool with towns like Abilene. Too many folks, too many herders, too much *mean* law." Hickok grinned. "Nebraska mebbe. The wagon trails. Mebbe I'll wander over toward Omaha. I hear the Pinkertons are about to open an office up that way."

"Watch your hair," Hickok said. "Got a letter

from my old pard Charlie Utter. Says the Indians are gettin' downright unfriendly." Preacher nodded. "By the way," Hickok said, handing Preacher a small package. "That's a little somethin' to tote with you. One day, you'll be facin' the same problem. Some newspaper man or story teller will catch up to you."

Preacher opened the package. It was a tintype photograph of Jim Hickok. He'd personally inscribed it.

    Preacher,

Keep your back to the wall.

    Your Pard,
    J.B. Hickok

Preacher rode from Hickok's office over to the Houston Emporium.

"You the type that doesn't backtrack his own trail?"

"No Luri," Preacher said. "I'm not. I'll get back to Abilene."

"Might let a girl know where you are, if you roost in one spot long enough. Who knows what might happen?" Preacher smiled. As Luri kissed him he got the vision again—Rosamonde—pressing a pistol to her breast, she fired it. Preacher blinked. Luri pulled away, looking quizzical.

"Goodbye, Luri," Preacher said. He stood, walked out and she hurried to the door and watched him until he was out of sight.

# 6

The summer of 1873, one of drought, locusts and unmericiful heat, gave way to a winter of equally ill repute. Preacher found himself caught in an early and particularly harsh blizzard, so he sought refuge in North Platte, Nebraska.

The Union Pacific hotel was the center of North Platte's activity. That activity was considerable and little hindered by the weather. Only the wagon train traffic along the California and Oregon trails was halted.

Trains now chugged east and west several times a day and North Platte was a major U-P center. It boasted a main passenger terminal, water and coal stop, and the largest engine shops on any rail line west of Omaha.

North Platte was often the site for meetings between Indian agents and those they were supposed to serve. The major peace conferences had been held there within the past two years and numerous plains tribes wintered there.

Wells-Fargo had a major stage depot in North Platte. Hundred of soldiers were a common sight, many either coming to or departing from Fort Kearney to the east. It was also the plains home of no less a personage than Colonel William F. Cody.

Frankly, Preacher was glad to be off the trail, bad weather aside. During the more than two years since he'd ridden into Abilene, Preacher had been mobile. He'd worked again with his friend Hickok, rode shotgun on several Wells-Fargo runs, rode assistant scout duty on two wagon trains, and did some dispatch riding for the army. He needed some rest and he was facing the prospect of replacing his big stallion, Cap'n. North Platte, he decided, would be his haven until spring.

About the only thing the man they called the Widow Maker hadn't done in that time was find Brock Sturgis and Joe Juniper. It wasn't due to any less activity on their part. They had robbed five stage coaches, four banks, one Wells-Fargo office, and were now believed to have been responsible for the theft of a large quantity of U.S. Army property. Several times during the period, once while in the company of Jim Hickok and Texas Jack Omohundro, Preacher nearly caught up with the duo. Again however, Sturgis and Juniper slipped the knot that was about to tighten around their necks.

Well rested after two days, Preacher emerged from his room and made his way to the Coal Tender, one of the two casinos in the Union Pacific hotel. He made his way to the bar and found it devoid of Teton Jack. He supplied the barkeep with his own last bottle. Preacher had also taken to smoking a pipe on occasion, a lead which was followed by Jim Hickok. Mostly, he smoked a coarse blend of black tobacco called Matchless. It was one of the prime chewing tobaccos of the day but Preacher found the taste to his liking and the aroma rather pleasant.

He was enjoying both pipe and whiskey when he was accosted by a young, stout looking man in finely tailored clothes.

"Forgive my intrusion, sir," the young man said, smiling, "but you are one hell of a difficult gentleman to corral."

"It's intentional," Preacher said. He eyed the man with a curious detachment, having established that the stranger was not armed.

"My name is Breed sir, Nathan Hale Breed."

"So you're Breed," Preacher said. He blew smoke toward the man. Breed's smile half faded. "I know men who would have hunted you down and shot you for a lot less lies than you've printed about me."

"It's my job," Breed replied. His voice was sharp and firm but his tone was somewhat defensive.

"Lying?"

"I meant reporting. Writing stories of interest to my eastern readers. Stories about the men who are opening this country up."

"And the truth be damned."

"Not at all, Mister Preacher."

"Don't call me mister. As a matter of fact," Preacher continued, "don't call me anything. Just leave me be Mister Breed." Breed inhaled, swelling his chest to maximum capacity. He pulled back his shoulders and tried to compete with Preacher's more than six feet in height.

"You're news, sir."

"No I'm not. I'll be news when somebody guns me down. You're making me news Breed, and I'll ask you to stop it."

"If you don't like what I write, or if it's not accurate, then set the record straight, Preacher. Tell it the way it really is."

"Go to hell," Preacher said. He set his glass back on the bar, tapped the tobacco from the stubby cherrywood pipe, and slipped it into his inside coat pocket. He then settled his hat on his head, straightened to his full height and walked away.

"I won't quit writing about you Preacher," Breed hollered. "I won't stop telling the stories, true or not. They're all I've got until you agree to talk to me." Preacher ignored the young reporter and found a table of Blackjack with a vacant seat. He took it.

"Jack Dillon," the dealer said, extending his hand. "If you're who the kid claims you are, I'm honored."

"Deal," Preacher said. He shoved ten dollars onto the table in front of him. An ace turned up. Preacher lifted the bottom card and peered, carefully. A king. Dillon went bust and paid double.

"I got no use fer a sneak thief bastard that makes his livin' shootin' down other men." The words came from a burly, older gent at the end of the table. "Cash me in." Dillon did, with one hand. He held a Deringer on the man with the other.

"You sit at my table, you make pleasant conversation, play cards and keep your opinions to yourself, or you don't play. You understand me?" The man shot a caustic but surprised glance at Dillon. He'd obviously expected to be backed by someone else. One gent just got up and left, chips forgotten. He smelled trouble and wanted no part of it. Another tensed but stayed put. The man with the opinion finally shrugged, glanced at Preacher and then turned and walked away.

"Sorry Preacher," Dillon said, replacing the Deringer in a tiny holster sewn into his vest. "You probably get plenty of that kind of talk. I can assure you, you won't get it at this table."

"I'm grateful," Preacher said, shoving his forty dollars out. "Now deal." Dillon felt a sting of resentment but he passed it off, smiled and dealt another round. Preacher stayed with 16 and Dillon went bust a second time.

Nathan Breed took the mouthy man's seat. He bet a dollar.

"Five dollar minimum limit," Dillon said. Breed swallowed, eyed Dillon, eyed Preacher, who ignored him and fished for more money. Dillon dealt. Preacher took a hit on a 15 and lost. Breed stayed on a 19. He lost too. Dillon hit 21.

"I believe," Breed said, after more than an hour's play, "that you are about to have company, Preacher." It was the first words spoken by anyone which Preacher acknowledged. He looked up, followed Breed's own line of sight and turned a little to his left. He saw a big man in a sheepskin coat walking toward the table. On the coat's left lapel was a tin star.

"Cash me in," Preacher said.

"Me, too," Breed echoed.

Preacher collected and stood up. The man arrived.

"I'm the United States marshal. Hank Coffey by name. You J.D. Preacher?"

"I am."

"I got a message for you, Mister Preacher." Coffey eyed the wiry gunman, shaking his head at Preacher's youth. "Goddam son, you don't look old enough to have killed forty men." Breed smiled. Perhaps the marshal could extract a printable reaction.

"What's the message," Preacher asked.

"Jim Hickok sent it. He and Mister Cody and some others are on their way here. They want a meeting. The message came from Fort Kearney. It said the meeting is army business."

"Thanks," Preacher said. He started to walk away.

"Just a second, bounty hunter." Preacher turned. Nathan Breed tensed. So did Jack Dillon. "I've been trackin' the Platte, the Republican and the Loup and the Niobrara Rivers for nigh on to five years now. Lookin' for Brock Sturgis and a man called Joe Juniper. One day, I'll find 'em. I can't stop you bounty huntin' Preacher, if I could, you can bet your ass I would. Meantime, I'll be askin' you to do your work outside my jurisdiction. That takes in all o' Nebraska."

"That it, Marshal?"

"Not quite. I'll tell you, right here, right now, speakin' to your face an' in front o' witnesses. I don't give a pinch o' cow dung for your kind, Preacher. You're a goddam blight on humanity. You get out o' line in my jurisdiction an' I'll come get you. You, Hickok, all of 'em, 'ceptin' Colonel Cody. You're a murderin' lot an' I'll have no truk with you an' no trouble from you."

"I'll remember that, Marshal. Good night now."

# TRAIL OF DEATH

Preacher turned and walked away. Dillon's eyes were on him. So were Marshal Coffey's. Nate Breed's eyes were on them. He smiled, sardonically.

"I think you made a mistake, Marshal," Jack Dillon said. "That man wouldn't hesitate to shoot you if you interferred with him, anymore than he'd hesitate about shooting Brock Sturgis."

"Or," Coffey said, casting a scathing glance at the well-groomed gambler, "a cheap tin horn." Coffey turned on his heel and stalked out. Dillon, obviously reacting to Coffey's barb, glanced up.

"This table is closed, gentlemen." Nate Breed smiled and walked to the bar. A minute or so later, Jack Dillon joined them. "I'll buy you a drink, Mister Breed."

"Thanks," Breed said. They sat in silence, sipping for a few minutes. It was Dillon who finally broke the silence again.

"That stuff you write about gunmen? Can't be *all* true." Breed sighed and looked up. "Hardly. I've reached the point where I don't know the difference anymore. Oh," he continued, smiling, "there's a grain of truth to all of it, but, well, I'd like to get all of the real truth."

"What you wrote about him," Dillon asked, pointing to Preacher who had taken a seat, alone, at a corner table, "how much of that is true?"

"Most if it. I mean, he had killed twenty three men by his twenty third birthday. Most of them were good men with guns and most deserved what they got."

"I heard he killed his own kin. That right?"

"Sure is, up in Colorado, his brother, Zachary."

"Gunned him in a fair fight?"

"So I heard," Breed replied. "But, much as I regret it, I wasn't there."

"You ever see him kill a man?"

Breed shrugged and shook his head. "Never have." He looked at the gambler. "I don't think I want to."

"Hell, why not? You're a reporter. You write a lot of manure about him and Hickok and their kind, but how many of them do you know for sure are really that good?"

"They are. Most of them anyway." Now Breed glanced toward Preacher. "I heard it said that Bill Hickok told Preacher he thought his gun handling was not human . . . something, you know, ghostly."

"You believe what you write?"

"I believe enough of it to know that I don't want to be on the wrong end of his gun." Breed looked into Jack Dillon's face. Nate Breed wasn't too old, nor had he been long in the west, but he had a sixth sense about men. The look he saw on Dillon's face, he didn't like. Dillon, Breed reckoned, was considering giving himself a go at J.D. Preacher.

"He'll kill you," Breed said. Dillon's head jerked around. He was frowning. "Do you think you're that good, that fast," Breed asked.

"I don't think that," Dillon said. His tone was flat, unconvincing. He got up. "Good night, Mister Breed." Nate Breed just nodded.

Jack Dillon was as smooth a card dealer and as sure a gambler as then reposed west of the big river. He'd earned an enviable sum of money and a respectable reputation in the past decade. He was thirty three, single, choosy about his female companionship, and he enjoyed a rapport with men on both sides of the law. He was also a shrewd businessman, and his business dealings usually bordered on less than respectable.

He waded through the snow and cold of North

Platte's main street, walked briskly along Third and looked in both directions before he entered the Buffalo saloon. It was located in the less affluent part of North Platte, on Railroad Street.

"Evening, Hy," he said to barkeep Hyatt Overjade. Hy nodded. "I'm looking for the Kid."

"He's upstairs with Lily." Dillon looked upstairs and then headed there. On the second door he came to he paused and knocked.

"Who the hell is it?"

"Jack Dillon. I need to see you Kid, it's . . . it's important."

"See me in the morning."

"It can't wait," Dillon said.

"What's it about?"

"Money, and a sure reputation." A moment later the door opened. Dillon smiled. A disgusted looking girl pushed her way by both men and the Kid motioned with his head for Dillon to come in. The Kid poured a whiskey and offered another to Dillon. The gambler declined. He took out his handkerchief and blew his nose, then rubbed it several times to remove the excess moisture which had built up from his walk to the saloon and whore house.

"Well? You busted in on me Dillon, for what?"

"You ever heard of a gunman they called Widow Maker?"

"Hell yes. Name's Preacher. Bounty hunter."

"Is he as good as they say?"

"I doubt it." The Kid downed another drink and then grinned. "Ain't *nobody* that goddam good."

"How about you?"

"I'm as good as they come gamblin' man, better prob'ly."

"Better than this . . . this fellow Preacher?"

"Sure."

"He's here," Dillon said, "in North Platte. He's over at the U-P, right now."

"I told you when I rode in gambler, I'm waitin' for my brother. I don't want no trouble in North Platte. I got a week to stay an' they's a U.S. marshal here."

"And if it's handled right Kid, you could ride out of North Platte . . . with your brother and about twenty five thousand dollars. That would be your share of what I figure a gunfight between you and this Widow Maker would bring."

The Kid was incredulous. He stared open mouthed at Jack Dillon. Finally he said, "That's a helluva lot o'money. How can you swing that much, gambler?"

"That's my worry, my end. You understand?"

"Twenty five thousand?" Dillon nodded. The Kid turned back to the dresser, poured another drink and then eyed himself in the mirror. He smiled. "And a reputation."

"A big one," Dillon urged, sensing he could close the trap he'd so carefully set. "I don't know if everything I've heard is true, but that man Preacher is one of the best. Gun him, nobody'd bother you, but," Dillon added, smiling, "everybody would respect you."

"Yeah." The Kid turned. "Let's go, gambler. You got a deal."

"Hold it, easy Kid. You don't rush these things. I've got to arrange the bets, the right odds, you know, set the stage. A day or two. Three at most. I think I can even get the marshal out of town."

"An' the sheriff? That sonuvabitch will come lookin' for me with a scattergun."

"I'll handle that too. You just make sure you stay out of sight. Just wait Kid, wait 'til I get back to you."

Jack Dillon was smiling to himself as he made his

way back to the Union Pacific hotel. Mentally, he could envision a gambling take of sixty to seventy thousand dollars from the showdown he had in mind. In winter, North Platte was the refuge for some of the wealthiest cattle, horse, stage and rail magnates in the west. Men to whom ten or fifteen thousand dollars was just a nice evening's win—or loss. Dillon had occasionally made some pin money dealing cards in a game or two with the likes of them, but he'd never been well enough off to match wits and chance against them. Now, he could promote something which would put him, finally, in the class for which he lusted.

Back at the hotel, Dillon sought out Priscilla Forshay. She was a sometimes dance hall queen, sometimes night lady, and at all times ready to capitalize on her considerable attributes.

She poured Dillon a drink, handed it to him, put her hands on her hips and said, "Well, tin horn, what scheme have you devised this time?" She knew all too well that Jack Dillon would not, otherwise, run the risk of being seen in her company.

"How many big spenders in North Platte right now?" he inquired.

She considered him. She smiled. "A dozen, mebbe two or three more than that. Why?"

"I can supply some action for them. The kind they all like."

"You mean like that pugilist you brought in two years back?" Dillon winced. The bare-knuckled fight which he had touted so highly never came off. It cost Priscilla nearly five thousand dollars and came very near to costing Jack Dillon his life.

"A gun fight."

"You bastard! Isn't there anything sacred to you?"

"Don't get moral on me," Dillon snapped. "You'd do it all yourself, if you could."

"Who do I have to bed down?"

"Maybe nobody, maybe a gun fighter named Preacher."

She laughed. "Preacher? Goddam, me in bed with a Preacher." She laughed.

"He's a bounty hunter with a helluva reputation. S'posed to be faster than greased lightning, better than Hickok even."

"An' you believe it?"

"I don't give a damn. He's fast enough. Most of the men you deal with have heard of him."

"An' who goes against this, uh," she thought about the name again and smiled. "Preacher?"

"The Cheyenne Kid." Priscilla was suddenly paying attention. She considered the gambler, recognized that he was serious, and acknowledged the revelation with raised eyebrows and a nod of her head. She was impressed. "He's in North Platte right now," Dillon said, "waiting on his brother to get here."

"I'd heard the Kid was dead."

"Well, he isn't."


The youth about whom Jack Dillon and Priscilla Forshay were talking was, in fact, Daniel Trent Bullock. He was the second born to Hawthorne Bullock of the Bullock Weapons Company of Richmond, Virginia. He had been weaned on guns, mostly pistols. The Bullock wealth had been shattered in the late war.

When Daniel turned eighteen, he rode west in search of his older brother Caleb. He found him in the spring of 1870. Caleb was under lock and key in a Cheyenne jail, three days away from a hangman's noose. He had been tried and found guilty of the rape and murder of two women.

Two dozen or more witnesses testified later that a mere boy, a boy none of them could identify, simply challenged the sheriff and four deputies outside the jail one morning. Their stories were hair-raising. After a verbal exchange, which included direct threats, the sheriff deemed it appropriate to place the youth under arrest.

The ensuing exchange of gunplay was unlike anything the witnesses had ever seen before, even in open, lawless and bawdy Cheyenne's early days.

Danny Bullock, blazing away with twin Colts, outdrew and outshot all five men. The sheriff died instantly, along with two deputies. Bullock escaped with a mere scratch, leaving the remaining deputies alive but out of action. One of them was crippled for life. Bullock then freed his brother, rode through the town shooting up store fronts in a final hurrah, and the deadly duo vanished.

Wanted posters, newspapers and even a pulp story or two appeared. Rewards were reaching the twenty thousand dollar level, but no one reported seeing Caleb Bullock or the Devil incarnate who had freed him. The pink faced youth was now known far and wide as The Cheyenne Kid.

The two holed up in Canada until the posters and the newspapers began to yellow with age. They slipped back into Montana territory, robbed several miners and some hapless wayfarers, but avoided any major attention. Finally, through old cronies, Caleb Bullock began to formulate a plan for the single biggest robbery yet perpetrated west of the Mississippi. He told his baby brother to stay out of sight. It was that plan which had finally led the Kid to North Platte.

"What's in it for me?" Priscilla finally asked.

"Ten thousand."

"*If* the Kid wins."

"He'll win," Dillon said, smiling. "I'll make sure of that."

"These gentlemen you want me to set up—they're not going to buy a pig in a poke."

"They won't have to. I'll see to it they get an ample demonstration of both men's skills."

"And if you can't?"

"Then nobody's the wiser and the bets are off."

"You are a bastard," Priscilla said.

"And you're a whore," Dillon shot back, but he smiled and added, "but there's no reason for either of us to be poor, is there?" The girl didn't reply.

# 7

The snow and cold didn't deter most of the populace of North Platte from venturing out two days later. Arriving on the westbound were half a dozen prominent gentlemen. Most of North Platte's residents came to the depot to gawk.

Coming home was the fabled frontiersman and buffalo hunter, William F. Cody. Buffalo Bill was surrounded by legends of even more outlandish proportions than those about Hickok or Preacher. Accompanying him was the chief Indian agent in the area, J.J. Saville. He would represent the interests of nameless men in the nation's capitol. Also debouching the special coach was Lieutenant-Colonel George Amstrong Custer, late of the great victory, as the eastern press had dubbed it, on the Washita. Behind him came Jim Hickok and Senator William B. Allison of Iowa.

After appropriate welcoming speeches and their responses, the party sought the warmth and comfort of the best suite of rooms the Union Pacific hotel could afford them. The railroad picked up the cost.

Jim Hickok introduced J. D. Preacher to the lot, and the men talked amiably about various subjects. It was finally Senator Allison who turned the conversation to the reason for the trip.

"As you, or some of you are aware, we have been experiencing considerable difficulty in the area of the Dakota territories known as the Black Hills. Trappers and miners have been claiming gold has been found."

"It's more than a claim," Cody said, "I've seen some mighty convincing evidence. Ore that could produce a hundred and fifty ounces to the ton, mebbe more."

"It is on Colonel Cody's evidence gentlemen that Washington has made its decision. We have ordered an expedition into the hills. It is scheduled for next spring and will be of such size and shape as to discourage the hostiles from interfering." Preacher frowned and the Senator took note of it. "A question, Mister Preacher?"

"Just plain Preacher, Senator, and I'll hold my question for the time being."

"As you wish, sir. Well then, Lieutenant-Colonel Custer here will lead the expedition. His entire Seventh Cavalry regiment will make the trek." Allison smiled. "I believe the Seventh's record alone will discourage opposition."

Agent J.J. Saville now opened a dispatch case, removed several papers and placed them on the table. "We wish to engage the services of several civilian scouts. Unfortunately, Colonel Cody is already obligated to other matters. Mister Hickok, as Chief scout, has already engaged two. I have here a government contract for you mister, uh . . . well . . . Preacher."

Preacher eyed Saville. He didn't like him, he'd heard stories. He knew some of them to be true. Saville was lining his own pockets at the expense of a hell of a lot of Indians. Preacher now glanced at Jim Hickok. Hickok recognized the expression.

"I'm not interested," Preacher said.

Cody spoke. "I'd take it as a personal favor if you'd accept. Jim speaks highly of you and he's agreed to ride in my place. I'd be obliged if you'd ride in his."

J.D. Preacher could count, on one hand, the men he'd met in the last five years for whom he would give more than a plug of horse dung. Cody and Hickok were two of them. Preacher's eyes met those of the famed plainsman. Preacher finally, albeit reluctantly, nodded.

"Good," Senator Allison said, beaming. "That's settled then. I'd like to ask all of you to be my guests for breakfast in the morning. At that time, we'll discuss more details of the expedition and the considerable preliminaries which must be done. Custer here will also have a report for you at that time."

The group dispersed, save for Cody and Hickok. It was Hickok who spoke first. "Thanks Preacher man."

"I don't like it," Preacher said, "not one damned bit."

"Neither do I," Cody said, smiling. "It's one more reason why I'd like you riding with Jim."

"What about the Indians? I don't know a hell of a lot about what's happened before," Preacher said, "it's not my usual line of work. But I recall something about those Hills, and a treaty."

"The treaty of Sixty-Eight," Cody said. "I was there. It gave the Sioux and their red brothers all of the Black Hills, in perpetuity. They won't take kindly to treading on the Paha Sapa."

"Paha Sapa?"

"Sacred ground," Cody said. "The Black Hills represent the center of the world to the plains tribes. The big chiefs go up there to palaver with Wakan Tanka, the Great Spirit. Their forefathers are buried there."

"The Indians? They know about this little expedition?"

"They don't. That's where I come in. I'm meeting with Red Cloud, Sitting Bull and some others."

"To ask, or tell?"

"Ask, Preacher. It was the only way I'd agree to help at all."

"What do you think of it, Jim?"

"I think we'd best have some good men along so that when it's over, we'll at least be able to know the truth is told."

"Permission or not, the Indians are going to get the wrong end of the deal again, aren't they?"

Hickok nodded. "Can't stop that, Preacher. Me'n Cody here been tryin' since about the time you were ten years old, back in the fifties. I hope we can help get 'em the best deal, but we can't stop what's happenin'." Hickok jabbed his finger at Preacher. "Neither can you."

"Mebbe not, but I don't have to like it and I don't have to participate."

"I believe you do," Cody said. "If we all take that attitude, we'll never see justice in this country."

"We're supposed to have justice now," Preacher retorted.

Cody smiled and shook his head, negatively. "No,

# TRAIL OF DEATH

son . . . we've got law now, but I've learned that *justice* is a little like a lame horse. Law rides in fast, arrives early, makes a lot of noise and then sits back and waits for justice to show up. Sometimes it's a long wait.'"

Cody said his good night and Preacher shared a final drink with Jim Hickok. "Who else is going to this party?"

"Scoutin' you mean?" Preacher nodded. "Colorado Charlie Utter an' Jack Omohundro."

"What's Cody think of Custer?"

"Thinks he's a little too puffed up with himself an' a little too disrespectful of the Sioux an' their friends."

"What do you think?" Hickok finished his drink and got up.

" 'Bout the same, but he's a fighter."

"You like him Jim, don't you?"

"I like him. You might too, time this little ride is over."

"Doesn't bother you the way we've treated the Indians?"

"No more or less than it bothered me the way Southerners treated Negroes."

"We didn't whip our Blacks. They ate good and lived with their own."

Hickok smiled and walked to the door. "Your daddy pay 'em, did he?"

Preacher winced. "No."

"He have white men workin' for 'im?" Preacher nodded. "He pay them?"

"I get your point, it's not the same."

"Why isn't it?" Hickok asked. "Only difference I see is the color."

"You've done in your share of red men, Jim."

"Yep, white too but not just because o' their color.

67

I may not be able to change nothin' that's goin' on, but I can't sit by an' do nothin' either."

Preacher pondered far into the night the words he'd heard from Cody and Hickok. Outside of Morgan Lake, the gambler who'd befriended him and passed on his gun skills to Preacher, the bounty man could think of no others for whom he felt so much respect. Still, he felt himself being tugged by an unseen force into a series of events he neither understood nor approved. It was another of the lessons from Preacher's book of life which seemed contrary to Preacher's law. He doubted that this particular conflict was one he could settle simply by his skills.

Preacher was up at first light and sipping coffee in the dining room of the U-P hotel several hours before the scheduled breakfast. He was surprised to find himself joined by gambler Jack Dillon.

"May I?" Dillon gestured toward a chair. Preacher nodded. "I'll come to the point quickly," Dillon said. "A friend of mine—a woman—does some, well, missionary work with a group of children. She is in need of some additional funds."

Preacher eyed Dillon suspiciously. He'd already spotted the man for a tin horn—good with his hands and his cards, but no professional in the same sense as was Morgan Lake.

"You don't strike me as a man concerned with such things, Dillon."

Dillon shrugged, arms extended, palms upward. "The lady is, shall I say, very convincing."

"How much?" Preacher reached for his money. Dillon's hands now shot out in front of him, palms toward Preacher.

"No, no sir. I wouldn't presume to merely solicit

cash, sir. In fact, I was rather hoping I could impose upon you to assist me and raise . . . well . . . a respectable sum."

"I don't follow you."

"I know that Colonel Cody and Wild Bill Hickok are both in North Platte, and I know that you are a friend. A demonstration of shooting skills," Dillon said, "would generate much interest and no small sum of cash."

"Sorry Dillon, those men don't use their guns in that fashion. Neither do I."

"Respectfully Preacher, but, well, I must disagree. My lady friend already approached the others, last evening. They did agree. It is set for tomorrow morning . . . at the depot."

"Cody and Hickok *agreed* to this?"

"I'll admit I was as surprised as you are but," Dillon nodded, "yes, they did. There are others too. Less skilled I'm sure, but they will all attract a crowd and, of course, some contributions."

"I'll be there," Preacher said. He didn't like it. He didn't like Cody or Hickok at the moment either. He was dragged into another incident which he felt carried the seeds of trouble.

Dillon had barely departed when Preacher found another intrusion of his privacy. This one in the form of Nathan Hale Breed.

"I've just spoken with that gambling gent, Dillon I think it is. He told me about tomorrow's little shooting match."

"More fodder for you, Breed."

"If you don't like it, why do it?"

"That's none of your business."

"A shooting match between Colonel Cody, Wild Bill Hickok, J. D. Preacher and God knows how many others, *not* my business?" Breed smiled. "My editor and publisher in New York could give you quite an argument on that opinion."

"Report the goddam thing Breed, but don't press me for *my* reasons for doing it."

"Cody gave me his—Hickok too."

Preacher stood up. "That's their business."

"I'll have to report something about the fabled Widow Maker, won't I?"

"Yeah Breed," Preacher shot back, "I imagine you will. Try something different this time."

"Like what?"

"How about the truth," Preacher said, walking away. Nate Breed again felt the pangs of frustration well up within him. Indeed, the feeling was a gnawing hunger to know more of this tall, brooding shootist. There was something about him which set him apart from men like Hickok, Cody and the others. That something, Breed knew, was the real J.D. Preacher.

The breakfast meeting was over. Preacher felt more ill at ease than he had the day before. He couldn't pinpoint the cause for it, but it was a crawling thing inside him—a foreboding which left in his mind more questions than answers.

Cody was to meet with the Indians somewhere along Wounded Knee creek in early March. Privately, Preacher was hoping the chiefs would unite against the expedition idea and refuse permission. That it must be sought was probably the single strongest point in the treaty of 1868.

After the shooting match in the morning, Cody was headed east. Hickok would ride back to Fort Kearney with the others. There would be another meeting sometime in March or April—just weeks in advance of the Black Hills trip—if the Indians agreed to the trip at all. Custer, Preacher reckoned

# TRAIL OF DEATH

silently, was barely able to contain his excitement. He had been out of the headlines too long, almost completely since the Washita fight. He lusted for the limelight.

Preacher found another internal struggle with himself over Custer, the man. The Lieutenant-Colonel was likeable, very much so. Preacher's own experiences in the war, particularly his time with Colonel Mosby, made him knowledgable enough to recognize Custer's considerable tactical skills. His organization of the largest expedition in the west since the Lewis and Clark trek was a masterful display of administrative skills. Still, something about Custer bothered the lanky Tennessean. He vowed to one day devote considerable time to engaging this enigmatic man in conversation.

Nate Breed was informed, none too politely, that the breakfast meeting was off-limits to the press. He would, he was told, be given the story at the proper time. Both Hickok and Cody, however, held nothing back where the shooting match was concerned. Breed hung on every word and then decided to pursue more about the origins of the idea.

About mid-afternoon, Breed stumbled into his most shocking revelation. The purported organizer of this highly touted display of gunmanship was a whore. He sought out Priscilla Forshay.

"You find it too unbelievable," she said, "that a woman who earns her livelihood from so questionable a profession could care about others?"

"Franky, miss Forshay, yes, I do."

"Have you conjured up any other reason for it?"

"Where does the money go, exactly?"

"Into the North Platte Bank and Trust Company vault, Mister Breed."

Breed smiled. "I meant, ultimately. Just who

benefits? I mean, I know what I've been told, but where are these children?"

"You'd like to meet them?"

"I would, and I'd like to visit further with both you and mister Dillon, with the children."

"That can be arranged," Priscilla said, coolly. "Are you staying at the Union Pacific?"

"Yes."

"Then tomorrow, right after the match, we'll arrange it."

"Why not *now*," Breed asked, skeptical about the delay.

"Because other matters are too pressing," she replied, turning to smile at him, "and you can get the children's reactions at the same time. You know, to what they will have just witnessed."

"Yeah," Breed said, nodding. "I guess that would be the best time."

Several blocks away from the U-P Hotel, Jack Dillon was drinking whiskey with the Cheyenne Kid.

"Once the contest is over, the bets will go down." Dillon poured two more drinks. "I've arranged for telegraph cables to come from Fort Kearney to both the sheriff and the marshal. At best, North Platte will be left a deputy or two."

"And how about tomorrow?" the Kid asked. "How the hell am I supposed to get away with shootin' tomorrow?"

"You don't. I'll handle that after the law is gone and just before the actual showdown. Besides, we've got to be certain that none of Preacher's friends are about. Hickok, Cody and their partners."

"I can handle any of 'em," the Kid said.

"Sure Kid, sure, but why take chances."

"You think I can't handle 'em?"

# TRAIL OF DEATH

"Easy, Kid. Hell, I'm not doubting your words but there's a lot at stake here. Let's keep it simple. You just take J.D. Preacher, that's all. Just him."

"When?"

"If everything goes on schedule, Saturday night at the Union Pacific Hotel."

"You look worried, gambler," the Kid said. "How come?"

"Your brother," Dillon replied. "Will he interfere?"

"He won't be here. I got a letter yesterday. He's been held up in Denver. Won't be here 'til Monday." The Kid grinned. "Just in time for the buryin', eh gambler."

"Yeah Kid, just in time."

Jack Dillon rode west out of North Platte right after he left the Cheyenne Kid. Few people paid him any mind. Those who did thought nothing of it—save for one. Nate Breed watched him, puzzled. What was west? Nothing about which Breed knew anything. And Jack Dillon was a saloon gambler, not a trail hand, not a horseman and definitely not a man who enjoyed the rigors of a cold, wintery horseback ride.

Dillon rode six miles west and then turned north. He dismounted finally, in front of a soddy built amid a stand of trees along the Platte river. A giant of a man, clad in buckskins, opened the door.

"What for you ridin' clean out here, Dillon? I don't owe you nothin'."

"I got work for you," Dillon said. The giant stepped aside and Dillon entered, quickly removing his coat, hat and gloves and warming himself by the old number ten. That done, he produced a quart bottle of whiskey.

"What kind o' work?"

"The kind you do best, Billy. Killin' something."

"Something?"

"A man. But it's got to be done real, real careful."

Jack Dillon explained his plan and informed the big man that he would receive five thousand dollars for his services.

"Your shot—it has to be timed just right. It has to be sure so that everybody there will have no doubt that the Cheyenne Kid killed Preacher."

"You do your part gambler, I'll do mine. An' I want half o' my money right now."

"Yeah Billy, I figured you would." Dillon produced an envelope and the big man opened it, counted its contents, smiled, nodded and stuffed the envelope in the pocket of a huge bearskin coat. "If there is any change or any problem, I'll get word to you," Dillon said, putting his coat and hat back on. "If you don't hear from me, be in North Platte Saturday afternoon by four o'clock. I'll get to you then."

"An' if'n it goes sour gambler, I keep what you jist give me anyways." Dillon winced but nodded. He mounted up and rode off, extra chilly at the thought of anything going wrong and angering the man with whom he had just dealt.

The giant in the buckskins was Bittercreek Billy Quint. He was nearly seven feet tall, weighed in at three hundred pounds and had earned Jack Dillon the first money he'd made after he rode into North Platte.

Dillon had staged a wrestling match between a gandy dancer named Burroughs and Bittersweet Billy. Just five minutes before the match was to begin, Burroughs doubled over and dropped dead.

The crowd was surly and getting downright ugly. Bittercreek saved both their asses. He announced he

## TRAIL OF DEATH

could bend double, a five foot length of Union Pacific rail. The bets went down and Bittercreek delivered. Once after that, Bittercreek and Jack Dillon set up a match between the giant and a big brown bear. Bittercreek won. Having proven his prowess once to often, Jack could get no more takers on anything involving Bittercreek Billy. None, at least, in town.

Toward the end of the preceding summer, Dillon wrangled a respectable sum out of the men on a wagon train. It was set up on the basis of Bittercreek Billy's prowess with a rifle. The bets went down on shooting out the eye of a buffalo at a hundred yards. Bittercreek missed by about two inches—but no one knew it. Dillon had bought himself the same kind of insurance he was now acquiring for the showdown between the Cheyenne Kid and J.D. Preacher. In this case, he knew Bittercreek's real skill was adequate. Preacher would die, the Kid would get the credit, and Jack Dillon would have a stake for his dream—a small casino of his own in far away San Francisco.

# 8

No one who'd read the North Platte Sentinel on the evening before the shooting match would have considered being anywhere else the next day. Also, Dillon had printed up handbills touting the event and hired two dozen school children to distribute them to nearby farms and ranches. He, along with Priscilla Forshay, personally dealt with the businessmen, cattle and horse buyers, and other barons of wealth. Obviously, they were aware of the ultimate goal of the match. Many had already committed to sizeable sums, but without having chosen a winner. They wanted to see the skills involved.

In addition to Cody, Hickok and Preacher, Texas Jack Omohundro, Colorado Charlie Utter, Bittercreek Billy and a score of other men participated. Dillon had been clever enough not to pit the men against one another so much as he did against their targets. He was shrewd enough to know that the spectators would draw their own conclusions and pick their own favorites—even in some cases where

# TRAIL OF DEATH

their favorites might not emerge as the best.

The rifle competition was clearly Cody's. Charlie Utter and Bittercreek finished in a deadheat tie for second place, although somewhat distant from the number one spot. The pistol competition was up for debate about a winner. Hickok's accuracy seemed dominant but J.D. Preacher's speed defied description. There was a third group who held that no clearcut winner could be determined. Regardless, the event raised money and no one was disappointed with what they had witnessed.

Friends bid each other farewell, the crowds cheered Hickok and Cody as they boarded the eastbound, Jack Dillon made a public and over zealous display of his gratitude and of turning the money to the bank president, R. W. Tidwell. Preacher slipped away at the earliest possible time and returned to his room. He was surprised at a knock on the door just an hour later.

"Come in," he said, his hand at the ready, near his hip. "The door's not locked." He got his first, close-up look at Priscilla Forshay.

"Hello, bounty hunter."

"What can I do for you?" Preacher asked.

She eyed him, boot toes to hat crown. "I'd guess a helluva lot." She closed the door. "I was told you don't drink."

"You were told wrong. I just don't drink bar whiskey."

"Sorry, it's all I've got."

"No matter, I don't drink that much and never before noon."

"Seems I'll have to find another way to express my gratitude."

"Dillon said enough for everybody, but you're welcome," Preacher said. "Is there anything else?"

"Damn, you're a cold-blooded bastard, aren't you?"

"Some think that."

"What do you think?"

"I think I like my privacy. How other folks see it is their affair."

"You don't much like what went on this morning, do you?"

"I don't."

"Not even to help kids?"

"Especially not to help kids."

"You're an odd one. You make a living with guns, and bad-mouth their use for something worthwhile."

"The kids forget the money. They don't forget the guns." Priscilla's eyes went from Preacher's vest holster to his hip and back again. She smiled. "Something wrong?"

"No, it's just that I've never known but one other man who wore a holster like the one on your vest—sewn in place I mean. Actually, he wore two also, but both inside his coat."

Preacher frowned. He too knew of only one other man who'd used that style. "What was his name?"

"Morgan Lake."

"Jeezus. You knew him?"

"Yes," Priscille replied and then added, "on a Mississippi river boat."

"When did you last see him?" She looked quizzical. "Please," he asked.

"A year, maybe two now," she replied, thoughtfully. She looked up. "In New Orleans."

"How did he . . . did he look?"

"Not good. Look Preacher, you know him? You lookin' for him? He got a price on his head, or what?"

# TRAIL OF DEATH

"I knew him. I knew he was dying. I've wondered about him."

She shrugged. "He may be dead by now. He told me he'd already lived longer than the medicine men gave him."

"You know him well?"

"Real well." She laughed. "We spent a lot of time in New Orleans."

"I'll buy your dinner," Preacher said, "in exchange for a little conversation about a common interest." Priscilla smiled, toyed with a button or two near the top of her dress and nodded.

Their dinner was interrupted only once, by young Nate Breed.

"I'd like to finish the conversation we had earlier," Breed said to Priscilla. "And I appreciate the chance to meet those kids you told me about. I'm sorry I doubted you. The bank president took me out to the house. I commend you. I'm just sorry you weren't there."

"So noted," Priscilla said. "I'll give you your interview Mister Breed, some other time." She looked at Preacher. Breed grinned, nodded, tipped his hat and walked away. Priscilla studied Preacher's face. "You don't like him much either, do you?"

"Not much."

"Well, I can't say as I blame you. I sure as hell wouldn't want a pulp book written about *my* work in that much detail." Preacher managed a half smile. They ate.

"You ever see Morgan Lake shoot?"

Priscilla sipped her wine, swallowed, wiped the corners of her mouth and said, "Only once. It was in Natchez, Mississippi. He was, well, kinda like a . . . a magician, you know?"

"Yeah, yeah, I do."

"Preacher, did Morgan Lake teach you?"

"Yes, he did." Preacher leaned back and fished for his pipe.

"May I," Priscilla asked. "I haven't packed a pipe for a man for a long time, but I used to be pretty good at it." Preacher shrugged and handed it to her. "I guess your knowing Morgan explains a lot of things to me. It sure does about your skills with six guns."

"I'd like to see him."

"Me too," Priscilla said, handing Preacher his pipe. She held out a match and he puffed. She waited for a reaction.

"You haven't lost your touch."

Preacher walked with Priscilla back to her room. He thanked her for her company and pondered what she would be like in bed. He didn't have to wait long to find out. When she next came to his room, she was wearing only a night gown. She said she wanted to ask him something as she stepped in and he closed the door. He turned around and she was naked.

"I don't buy women anymore," he said.

"I'm not selling." She walked to him, thrust her arms around his neck, pressed her body to him and kissed him. That done, she moved to his bed, laid down and waited.

Preacher's needs were all too often neglected, if not forgotten completely. He worked at a life and death trade and he could rarely afford to neglect or forget that. He stripped and when Priscilla saw him, she gasped. He turned the lamp down and slipped onto the bed beside her.

"You're a lot of man in more ways than one," she whispered.

# TRAIL OF DEATH

Preacher kneaded her breasts. They were full, firm and very sensitive to his touch. He replaced his fingers with his lips and Priscilla's lithe body tensed under his ministrations. He shifted his position and let his tongue trace a path along the underside of her breasts, down her right side, across her abdomen and down, further and further.

Priscilla entwined Preacher's dark, softly waved hair around her fingers and closed her eyes. She imagined herself with him under other circumstances and with other motives. She felt a little queasy at her blatant approach to him. The feeling puzzled her.

She grew moist and passionate under his touch and finally tugged at the sides of his face. He slid upwards and positioned himself above her. She reached down and closed her hand around his hardened manhood, then stroked. He kissed her and again sent tingling sensations through her entire body with his tongue. A few minutes later Priscilla pushed on his chest, a signal for him to let her up. He did.

She repositioned herself on the bed, on her hands and knees. Preacher got to his knees and positioned himself behind her. He reached beneath her and began stroking her breasts. They swayed from side-to-side as her body alternately relaxed and then stiffened with the passion of Preacher's touch. He spread her labia, fingered her gently and then thrust himself into her most intimate recesses. Priscilla moaned and together they gave each other the ultimate in human pleasure.

Saturday morning, the 19th day of December, 1873, dawned bright and clear. It was cold in North Platte but promised a break in the bitterness of the past few weeks. A south wind, with just a hint of Texas in it, blew across the stock pens and filtered down along the main streets.

The man in black ate his breakfast, returned to his room and began the weekly process of cleaning his weapons. He had added two since he'd ridden in from Denver. There, he'd acquired the matched pistols upon which his life very often hung. They had been fashioned by an old German gunsmith and proved, as he'd told Preacher they would, to be the forerunners of many of the weapons to be produced by the major manufacturers. They were .44-.40 calibre, short-barreled. Smith and Wesson Company was now advertising similar pistols and the Colt Company was rumored to have some in production.

Preacher had purchased from Colt a custom manufactured killer. It replaced the old .58 calibre which had been given to him by his father. A pistol-carbine it had been called. The old Denver gunsmith had improved it but the Colt's weapon was even deadlier.

It was an over-under model with an eight shell magazine. Five for the upper barrel and three for the lower. It was a lever action with a hammer which could be operated with the thumb. To date, Preacher had not used the man-killer.

Preacher had also purchased a Rider magazine pistol. While similar to a Deringer, it was a much improved weapon. It was a .32 calibre, rim fire, five shot pistol which weighed only ten ounces. Usually, Preacher carried it in his left-hand vest pocket. The barrel was but three inches in length. Like the pistol-carbine, Preacher had found no use for the little gun. Still, both Morgan Lake and the old Denver gunsmith had urged him to keep abreast of the newest weapons. After all, for J.D. Preacher,

# TRAIL OF DEATH

they were his stock-in-trade.

As Preacher worked over his guns, reporter Nate Breed finished his breakfast and decided it would not be inappropriate to make a call on Priscilla Forshay. His knuckles were but an inch from her door when a familiar voice caught his ear—from inside the room.

" . . . but he won't do it for anybody but you, Priscilla."

"Oh yes he will, Jack. If Breed's story is even half true, J . D. Preacher will turn into a raging lunatic if he thinks some woman's tongue is going to be cut out."

Nate Breed's brow wrinkled up. He pressed closer to the door.

"But why not you? That time in bed soften you up?"

"Get out Jack! Get the hell out and go do what you started out to do. Get it over with."

"As soon as Bittercreek gets to town, Priscilla." Nate heard footsteps. "And you remember. You get Preacher outside—out in the open where Bittercreek has a clean shot, just in case.

"There's no just in case to it," Priscilla said. "I really did know Morgan Lake, at least by reputation. If he tutored J.D. Preacher you'll be damned lucky if the man doesn't kill the Cheyenne Kid and Bittercreek."

Nate Breed's head was swimming with what he'd heard. Preacher had been set up. Breed didn't know exactly how. Even the why was somewhat puzzling, simply because of the participants. One thing only was certain. Preacher was to be ambushed.

Nate got no answer when he pounded on Preacher's door. He hurried downstairs but met with more frustrations. No one had seen the tall, quiet man named Preacher. He may have left the hotel but Nate could find no one who could say for sure.

Jack Dillon came downstairs. When he reached the main floor of the hotel, he walked to the desk, barely nodding at Nate Breed. He spoke in low tones to the desk clerk, nodded and entered the Gandy Dancer's Hall, the second and largest of the hotel's casinos. Nate Breed hurried to the desk.

"Is Mister Dillon getting up a game by any chance?"

"Why, yes sir . . . he is. It is for . . . well sir . . . a person had best be very well heeled if he wishes to sit in the game." Nate nodded. He'd best take a seat in the lobby and wait.

Over the next quarter hour, half a dozen well dressed men entered the casino. Nate recognized one or two of them. When two more entered the lobby a few minutes later, pausing to chat near the casino's entrance, Nate worked his way into a position where, once again, he could eavesdrop.

"Powell wants another side bet," one of them said. "I can't cover it but he's betting on this man they call the Kid."

"I'll stake you Henry, if that's what you want, but I won't commit until this young gunman has shown me something impressive."

"Anytime now," the first man said, pointing toward the door. Nate looked. There was a boyish looking character wearing a full-crowned stetson and a heavy, sheepskin coat. He removed the coat and Nate saw the two gun rig. He'd heard about this boy—the Kid to whom Jack Dillon and Priscilla Forshay referred. The Kid Nate had read about a few years back. It all came together. This was the Cheyenne Kid. He was in town to gun J.D. Preacher.

# TRAIL OF DEATH

The two wealthy men disappeared into the Gandy Dancer's Hall. The Kid followed a moment later.

"Mornin' Miss Priscilla." Nate's hand jerked toward the voice. A man stood at the foot of the stairs, looking up. Nate looked up and there stood Priscilla Forshay.

A shot!

Nate nearly broke his neck getting into the casino. Jack Dillon stood near the bar where he tossed a white poker chip into the air. The Cheyenne Kid drew, fired and the chip disappeared. Priscilla Forshay walked up.

"Mister Breed," she said. Nate nodded. They both watched as Dillon tossed two chips, one with each hand, high into the air. The Kid drew both guns, fired and both chips were hit.

"Gentlemen," Jack Dillon said, gesturing toward a table. The wealthy looking, well dressed men flocked around him. Most held large sums of money in their hands. Priscilla Forshay excused herself, pushed by Nate Breed and a moment later, joined the crowd at the table.

Suddenly, the whole picture formed itself clearly in Nate Breed's reporter's mind. The shooting match, minus the Cheyenne Kid, a demonstration of the Kid's prowess and some heavy betting.

Nate turned just as three saloon girls, all smiling at him, walked by and entered the Gandy Dancer's Hall. Nate knew everything now. He recalled the many stories about J.D. Preacher. He particularly recalled the one about Preacher's sister and Quantrill's men raiding the Preacher plantation in Tennessee. One of those men had raped the gunman's sister—after he cut out her tongue.

A bell hop approached Nate. "Excuse me sir, but the desk clerk told me you were wondering about the whereabouts of Mister Preacher."

"Yes, yes I was."

"The livery, sir. He asked me to see to it his laundry was taken care of and he told me he was going to the livery stable."

"Where . . . which way?"

"East, sir. To the end of the street and then left about two blocks. You can't miss it. Jeremiah Teasley's Livery is what the sign reads." Nate Breed was already half-way to the door.

As he hurried out, Jim Kellett entered. Nate Breed might have stopped had he seen Kellett's tin star. He didn't. Kellett was one of two deputies still in North Platte. The evening before, telegraph cables had come from Fort Kearney. They requested, urgently, the presence of the United States Marshal and North Platte's sheriff. Accompanying them were three more deputies. The cables indicated the presence at Fort Kearney of three members of a gang which had robbed a North Platte bank more than a year earlier. North Platte was nearly wide open on this Saturday morning.

Gunshots had attracted Jim Kellett's attention. He had just begun his morning rounds. He felt a little guilty about being late that morning but he had just fathered his first child—a boy. He'd spent some extra time at home, watching his wife feed the baby.

"Mornin', Charlie," Jim said to the desk clerk. Charlie nodded and pointed toward the Gandy Dancer's Hall. "What's going on?"

"I don't know, Jim, an' I don't intend to go in there and ask." Jim smiled, understandingly. He turned and walked into the casino.

"Deputy," Josh Guthrie said, smiling, "everything is fine. Just a little demonstration of some shooting skills here. No trouble." Jim Kellett looked around. Some of the businessmen huddled over a table straightened and turned to eye the intruder. Josh Guthrie owned the casino. If he didn't have a complaint, Jim Kellett wasn't needed. The men in the suits had stepped back a bit. Jim Kellett saw Priscilla Forshay, Jack Dillon and the back of a young man who was wearing a double gun rig. Kellett frowned.

"You there, you with the guns." The young man turned, smiling.

"You talkin' to me, deputy?" Kellett's eyes grew large and round. By chance, he'd spent two days, not more than a month ago, ridding the sheriff's files of some old dodgers. Among them was one with a rough sketch and description of a young gunny wanted in Cheyenne.

"What's your name?" Kellett asked.

"Kid will do, the Cheyenne Kid." Jim Kellett's right hand jerked toward his hip. Almost at the same moment, a tiny red spot appeared on the front of his shirt. The red spot grew in size even as the deputy fell backwards into a table. His body hung there for a moment and then toppled to the floor.

"This wasn't part of the plan," Priscilla said.

"Shut up." Jack Dillon looked at the door. The desk clerk and a bell hop were both staring inside. They turned and hurried away.

"Anymore law in town," the Kid asked Dillon.

"Another deputy," The Kid grinned. "We got to get the bounty hunter in here . . . fast."

The bounty hunter had taken a different route when he left the livery. He stopped at Howard Galt's mercantile store and bought five boxes of .44-40 ammunition. He was just leaving the mercantile as Nate Breed entered the livery stable. Nate had walked very fast to get to the stable. When he left it, headed back to the Union Pacific Hotel, he was running.

Preacher rounded the corner and started the last half a block back to the hotel. He paused for just a moment when he saw one of the hotel's bell hops running off toward the sheriff's office. Preacher resumed his pace, a little faster. A man exited the tonsorial parlor across the street, paused, looked at Preacher and then trotted across the street and disappeared into the hotel. Preacher frowned, something was wrong, he could sense it. His eyes began to scan the buildings on the opposite side of the street. Ground level first, then the second floor windows. He saw nothing.

Preacher was about half the distance to the hotel's entrance when a girl burst through the doorway. She was screaming. Behind her, holding her by one arm, was a young man. The two ended up in the middle of the street. Priscilla Forshay came out, and she was also screaming. She looked in the other direction, then back. She saw Preacher.

"Stop him! He's going to cut her tongue out." Priscilla was pushed into the snow. Jack Dillon emerged and behind him, a knot of well dressed men. Preacher put the ammunition boxes on a window ledge and flicked the hem of his frock coat back. He stood on the board sidewalk, his eyes flitting up and down the streets but never staying long away from the young man and the girl. She was now cowering at the man's feet. Preacher saw no knife. The man was looking straight at Preacher.

The two shots which sounded even louder than usual in the icy, morning air, turned everybody's heads. They came from the opposite end of the street.

"Preacher! It's an ambush! The roof . . . the roof over the barber shop!" Preacher could identify Nathan Hale Breed. The gun from inside his coat barked once. The bullet went through Bittercreek Billy's head. At that, the huge body seemed frozen in place. Bittercreek, at the sound of the shots, had stood up. He made an easy target. Now, all three hundred pounds of him fell forward. His body smashed through the wooden roof overhang in front of the barber shop. There was a sickening thud, even in the snow, when it struck.

"You four-flushin' son-of-a-bitch," the Cheyenne Kid screamed. He kicked at the girl, drew and fired. Jack Dillon died instantly, a bullet through his brain. The Kid did a one and a half trigger spin with his pistol, holstered it and walked to the center of the street. "First bastard that so much as blinks will join Dillon. You hear me?" Most of the men within earshot nodded. In fact, The Kid was not interested. None of them were gunmen. He wasn't worried. His eyes never left Preacher.

"I had nothin' to do with that bastard on the roof, bounty hunter. That goddam Jack Dillon didn't believe I could take you. He did it. I don't need no bushwhacker backin' me."

Nat Breed had been paralyzed where he'd stopped. Now, suddenly, there was blood in his veins again. Reporter's blood. He dropped the gun he'd borrowed from a passer-by, ran to the shelter of a nearby doorway and peered around the corner of it to witness the next act.

Preacher holstered his gun, turned slowly and picked up the ammuniton boxes. He stacked them and with his left hand gripping the bottom one, pressed the others next to his body. He started walking.

"Pull on me, Widow Maker. Let's finish it." Preacher kept walking. Priscilla Forshay got to her feet. Preacher's eyes seemed to be burning through her flesh and into her very soul.

"My God . . . I'm sorry," she yelled, "I'm sorry Preacher."

"Pull on me bounty man, or I'll kill you where you stand." Preacher kept walking. He reached the door of the hotel and stopped.

At the corner, from the end of the street where Nat Breed had fired his warning shots, the hotel's bell hop now appeared.

"The deputy won't come . . . he won't come, he's too yella." The Cheyenne Kid laughed. "Seems to be a regular epidemic of yellow in North Platte all o' the sudden." His face contorted into a look of pure hatred. He focused it all on J.D. Preacher. "I'm tellin' you one more time bounty hunter, pull on me."

"You gentlemen," Preacher said, his voice emerging from between clenched teeth, "had best go through Dillon's pockets and retrieve your money. I'm assuming you bet on this little farce. The bets are off." Preacher wheeled suddenly and disappeared into the hotel.

"Preacher! Look out!" The voice was faint, distant. Nonetheless, Preacher recognized it as belonging to Nate Breed. He smiled. Just inside the door, he stepped to his right, drew his hip pistol, gripped it by the barrel and waited. A moment later, the Cheyenne Kid burst through the door.

"Hey," Preacher said. The Kid turned. Preacher laid the pistol butt over the Kid's head after flicking the Kid's hat off with his left hand. The Kid crumpled into a heap at Preacher's feet. The tall bounty man retrieved the Kid's pistols, tucked them in his waist belt and stepped outside.

"Tell the deputy it's over and he can come take his prisoner to jail."

Preacher hung his coat in the closet, laid the Kid's guns on the chiffonier and moved over to his bed. A knock turned his head. "It's Nate Breed."

"It's open."

"Why didn't you kill him?"

Preacher eyed Breed, smiled a little and shook his head. "You get it all written down, did you?"

"Why Preacher?"

"I'm grateful to you." Preacher cocked his head, scratched at the back of it and then looked up. "Even obliged."

Nate Breed's face was flushed. He was tired of being ignored. He had high cards now. He decided it was time to play them. "You *owe* me J.D. Preacher. I saved your hide."

"Mebbe. It would have been close enough, either way, to have been uncomfortable. You get any approval for your request to accompany Custer into the Black Hills next spring?"

"Of course not. The government is sending somebody in. It's not right." Nate frowned. He was angry with himself. Now *he* was answering questions again. "What in the hell does that have to do with anything?"

"I'll see to it you can ride in with me." Nate Breed's jaw dropped. "You write the truth, everything we see, everything we find that is, if the Indians allow it."

Nate rather flopped into a nearby chair. "Are you *serious*?"

"Like I said Breed, I'm grateful to you. Sometimes, I'd like you to tell me what you found out, how," Preacher grinned, "and when too, although that seems to be pretty obvious."

"Yeah," Nate said. "I cut it close, that's for sure." He looked up. "I still can't figure why you didn't kill the Cheyenne Kid."

"Well," Preacher said, "we'll be together for a few weeks. Mebbe you'll find out."

# 9

The snow was coming down in big, fat flakes. Two women from the First Presbyterian Church circulated among the customers in the dining room of the Union Pacific Hotel. They were collecting donations to help the needy. It was four days until Christmas. Preacher, just finishing off his breakfast, handed one of the women a fifty dollar bill.

"May the Lord bless you sir." Preacher smiled and nodded. "Are you a resident of North Platte sir?"

"No ma'am."

"If you are spending the holiday here alone, you are most welcome to come to our church on Christmas eve. It's the Presbyterian Church." She pointed off to the northeast. "The one with the big, tall steeple."

"I'm grateful," Preacher said.

"You look to be such a fine young man. Where are you from?"

"Lots of places, ma'am." Preacher was feeling nervous, ill at ease with a woman like this one. His most recent female company and conversation had certainly been a far cry from church talk.

"I meant, where were you born?"

"Tennessee."

Preacher saw someone enter the dining room, stop and look around. He leaned to one side to see around the woman. He saw Marshal Hank Coffey, and Coffey saw him. He started toward the table as Preacher got to his feet. The woman turned and saw the marshal. She smiled.

"Pardon me, ma'am," the marshal said. His look somewhat frightened the woman, so she stepped back. Coffey thrust two fingers into his shirt pocket, withdrew a tin star and tossed it onto the table. "Put it on, gun fighter. You're a deputy, by court order."

"Sorry marshal but . . ."

"No buts, bounty hunter. I know what happened, and I know why, mostly anyways. I can't figure you not gunnin' the Kid, but me an' the sheriff appreciate that you didn't. That is unless you knew."

Preacher frowned and considered Marshal Coffey, "Knew what?"

"That the Kid's brother an' half a dozen fast guns are comin' in today. Roundin' up enough men for a posse is tough enough when all they have to do is track somebody. Facin' these bastards is . . ." The marshal cut himself short, forgetting the presence of the woman from the church. He looked at her but there was not much to say. She offered a forced, half smile, stepped back and then covered her mouth and hurried off.

# TRAIL OF DEATH

"It's not my fight," Preacher said. Hank Coffey's head jerked back toward Preacher. He stepped closer, almost nose to nose.

"I've got one deputy, the sheriff has only got one, an' there's no time to round up anybody else. Me'n Sheriff Tomkin rode like hell to get back here when we found out what happened an' that them telegraph cables were phonies. I figure none o' that would have happened if one self servin' sonuvabitch named J.D. Preacher hadn't o' been in North Platte, Nebraska. It's your fight, alright."

Marshal Coffey then produced a paper from his pocket. He unfolded it and thrust it in Preacher's face. It was the court order, signed by the circuit judge, and naming J.D. Preacher as a deputy U.S. marshal for a period not to exceed seven days. By law, Preacher would receive five dollars a day and reimbursement of any out of pocket expenses.

"You refuse to comply with this order bounty man, an' I'm authorized to place you under arrest and detain you, in a jail cell, for not more than the period of time stated." Coffey smiled. "You'll also be charged with contempt of court." Coffey folded up the order, tossed it down next to the tin star and then added, "I'm half hopin' you'll turn me down."

"Marshal." Both Coffey and Preacher looked toward the door. Jack Omohundro stood just inside it. "Bullock and five men are out at the stock pens. Hickok asked me to ride back and find out what was going on. I tried to catch up to you yesterday. When I couldn't, I figured you were in a hell of a hurry. I just left the sheriff's office and the deputy told me what was going on. So I figured you'd want to know about those fellas at the stock pens. I rode by 'em comin' in." Omohundro smiled. "Lo, Preacher."

"Jack," Preacher said. He picked up the badge and held it up. "You pinning one of these on?" Jack nodded. "Alright Coffey. You've got yourself one more man."

Coffey looked at Preacher—a look of almost hatred. He nodded.

"They'll be too smart to try a straight bust out. What do you figure," Coffee asked Jack.

"Pull the Kid out of his cell, hog tie 'im to a horse and ride out to meet 'em. It's a quick way to find out just how bad they want the Kid, an' how anxious he is to die if they don't want 'im at all."

"I can't do that, Jack, an' you know it."

"What's stopping you marshal?" Preacher asked. "They're making the rules. Let's play by them."

"We do that an' we're no better'n them. Goddam it, I been a lawman most o' my life. I did it so's this kind o' shit would stop. I'll be Goddamned if some two-bit gun hand is going to erase all that." He looked straight at Preacher. "An' it's no never mind to me whether he happens to be wearin' a badge at the moment or not."

"I'll put on your badge marshal, but I won't commit suicide for you. We've got an edge, we're holding what they want. Use it."

"I'll use it. My way, the law's way." Coffey looked at Jack. "We'll meet at the jail an' wait 'em out." He turned back to Preacher. "That's an order. I'll expect both of you in fifteen minutes." Coffey stalked out.

"He's a good man Preacher, a damned good man," Texas Jack said, shaking Preacher's hand.

"I'll take your word for it Jack, but that won't keep him alive any longer."

"He lives by the law—or his interpretation of it anyhow."

# TRAIL OF DEATH

"That," Preacher said, "I'll give him. I do the same. Mine's called Preacher's law. Shall we ride to the stock pens?"

Preacher detoured only long enough to pick up his Colt's pistol-carbine. He loaded it, slipped on his heavy coat, and he and Jack Omohundro walked to the livery. Ten minutes later, they rode toward the stock pens.

Marshal Hank Coffey made three more stops in North Platte that morning. Then, he hurried back to the sheriff's office. What he found turned his stomach. Sheriff Tomkin and his deputy were both dead—their throats had been cut. The Cheyenne Kid was gone. A few minutes later, Ole Gerhensson, a carpenter, walked into the office. He was ghost white.

"Ole?"

"He was an Injun, big fella. Your deppity's at my place, dyin'."

Hank Coffey found Frank Lilly on the floor of Ole's workshop. He too had been cut up with a Bowie. He knew he was dying and there were tears in his eyes. "Injun Tom . . . I let 'im in . . . he's with 'em. I got a shot off. I think I hit 'im." Hank Coffey wiped his eyes and his nose. He'd been riding with Frank Lilly for twelve years. Injun Tom was a half breed buffalo hunter for the railroad. Coffey had always figured him for a friend, but a year back he'd been arrested after a fight in a North Platte saloon. Coffey testified in his behalf, but he jury didn't like Indians. Injun Tom didn't forget.

"Make him as comfortable as possible," Hank told Ole. Ole nodded. The marshal hurried back to the sheriff's office, loaded two shotguns and the sixth chamber of his Colt's. That done, he sat down at his desk to await the arrival of Jack Omohundro and J.D. Preacher. He sipped coffee, and he pondered Preacher's words. His mind's eye flashed to the bodies of the sheriff, the deputy, and his own friend dying a half a block away. He looked toward the cell where he placed the two bodies. Tears filled his eyes. Somehow, in some twisted way he thought, Preacher was right. Those men made the rules. The law would have to be bent at times to make it fit.

Preacher and Jack Omohundro dismounted, and tethered their horses to a rail just outside the office at the stock pens. Jack slipped a Winchester from its saddle boot. When Preacher removed both his heavy coat and his Prince Albert the cold air bit into his arms. He slipped the pistol-carbine from his bed roll and levered a heavy calibre shell into the upper chamber.

"Which end, Jack?"

"I'll take the south end. See you back at the sheriff's office." Preacher nodded and watched Jack Omohundro walk away. Preacher turned north and walked along the pen rails. So far, neither man had seen any signs of life. Preacher knew it was out there somewhere. Also, he knew this was no gun fight. No face to face, man to man confrontation. He would kill as quickly and as efficiently as he could. His mind wandered back to his home, to Bradburn Hill, Tennessee and his father's tales of the last day at the Alamo. The Mexicans had sounded the *Deguello*—ask no quarter, give none!

U.S. Marshal Hank Coffey was stirred from his bitter thoughts, and frowned as he fished for his pocket watch. "Goddam them!" He leaped to his feet, exited the office and mounted his horse.

"Marshal." Hank Coffey recognized the voice at once. His stomach tightened and his throat went dry. Suddenly, he leaned foward, pressing his torso

# TRAIL OF DEATH

and head tightly against his mount. He spurred the chestnut mare just as a shot rang out, then another. The second one caught the marshal about half way up the backside of his right arm. It missed the bone but struck his horse in the neck. She jerked, whinnied, staggered and Coffey anticipated her. He grabbed for his rifle and rolled to the right—off his horse and into thin air.

Another shot, and still another. Marshal Coffey's bulk smashed through a hitching rail and he landed on his back. His head whipped backwards and smacked into a stanchion. He levered a shell into his rifle, lowered the barrel and fired, levered and fired again. He rolled.

The next shot hit him. It burrowed into the cheek of his right buttock and he winced as the stabbing pain shot through his body. He scrambled along the board walk on his hands and knees, half pushing his rifle ahead of him. He heard heavy boots, stopped and looked up. He was looking into the menacing face of Injun Tom.

The shotgun blast nearly deafened Hank Coffey. He gauged the blast mentally—years of experience coming into play—as two barrels discharged almost simultaneously. His rifle was protruding in front of him now and half pointed upwards, but he knew it was too late to save him. Suddenly, he was looking at what was left of the top of Injun Tom's head. His body had crashed forward, inches from Hank's. Behind the Injun stood Ole Gerhensson.

"Jeezus Ole, get down!" A pistol barked once, again, again! Ole's eyes got big, he staggered with the first hit. His body flew through the air, backwards, with the impact of the others. Hank Coffey scrambled over top of Injun Tom's body and rolled through the open door of Ole's shop. Another shot splintered the wood just above Hank's head.

It was odd, but all the marshal could think was that Ole was single. His death wouldn't be so tough. Jeezus! What a sad thing to think. Hank could see Ole's boots. The old Swede saved my worthless hide, Hank whispered to himself mentally. He struggled to a kneeling position, his faced grimaced with the pain of movement which put stress on the wound in his butt.

"I'll have a tough time explaining a bullet in my ass," he said out loud. He peered cautiously around the corner of the counter. He could see nothing, hear nothing. Somewhere out there, waiting, was the Cheyenne Kid.

Preacher worked his way along the high board fence which was quickly running out. Thereafter, a three level log fence ran around the big main pen. There was no cattle, the snow inside the pens was virgin, save for bird tracks. Occasionally, a mound of snow indicated the location of a now frozen cow chip.

The log fence ran along for fifty yards. Off to Preacher's left there was a dozen or so watering tanks. Most were metal, all would afford a hiding place for a man—if he was in the prone position. He kept a sharp eye along the line of the tanks.

Preacher reached the end of the board fence. He'd all but forgotten the cold, but now he was reminded of the fact that he was without a heavy coat. A gust of wind whipped around the solid surface of the board fence and struck him full in the face and chest. He gasped and shivered. Two shots rang out far behind him. A rifle! Jack Omohundro was engaging the enemy.

"Heeya . . . heeyah!" Preacher heard the horse's

# TRAIL OF DEATH

hooves and the rider's shout. He crouched, pivoted to his right, eyed the open pen and fired. The heavy calibre slug tore into the man on the horse, lifted his body almost straight up and then threw it backwards. Preacher levered another shell into the chamber. A rifle shot took Preacher's hat off. He made a half turn and fired, levered and fired again. A second man went into the air, screaming.

Three hundred yards south of him, Jack Omohundro had been forced to seek refuge in a watering trough. Two or three inches of water had remained on its bottom, but it was now frozen solid and the cold began to penetrate Jack's outer clothing.

Jack had lost the heel of his left boot when he dived into the trough. He was fortunate it was all he'd lost. He'd been caught in the open, flat-footed, like a goddamn greenhorn. He managed one shot but hit nothing. Now, he was aware of at least three men who, by their positioning, had him in a crossfire. He couldn't return fire without exposing himself.

There was a sudden volley of gunfire. Bullets ripped into the trough, splintering wood and whining as they ricocheted from knots or spots strengthened by the presence of ice. Jack didn't move, and pressed himself tightly against the ice as he waited. Silence. He strained to hear the sound of footsteps but there were none.

A few moments later, he heard crunching snow in the distance, the snorting of a horse. One animal, then two galloped away. Jack Omohundro removed his hat, slipped his knife into his hand, put his hat on its point and raised it slowly above the edge of the trough. A shot rang out. The hat flew off to his right, so the gunman was to his left. Jack raised up and propelled himself over the edge of the trough and behind the side opposite the direction from which the shot had come. Another shot, then another struck the trough near his head. Jack raised, aimed and fired. The gunman, in the open near a barn, groaned, staggered and fell.

Jack looked north. Preacher waved and gestured with his weapon off toward town. Jack ran toward their horses where they met.

"I got two."

"You're one up on me," Jack said. There were no more words. Preacher and Texas Jack rode, hell bent, for North Platte.

Nearly a quarter of an hour had passed since Hank Coffey sequestered himself behind the counter in Ole Gerhensson's carpentry shop. His ass hurt and he could feel the warmth of the blood trickling down the back of his leg and the back of his right arm. He felt nauseous.

"You're a dead sonuvabitch lawman." Hank winced in pain as he jerked to the sound of the voice. He cursed under his breath and brought his rifle to a position where he could fire it. It hurt too much.

"Goddam," he said. He dropped the rifle and pulled his Colts.

"I'm comin' in, Marshal." The Cheyenne Kid had a pistol, fully loaded, in each hand. He levelled them at the window, just above the counter behind which Hank Coffey reposed. Alternately, he began to fire. 1—2—3—4—5—6—7—8. The window disappeared in a crystalline cloud of glass shards, tinkling down atop the counter and dropping onto Hank Coffey's head, coat, arms and hands.

During the fusillade, the Cheyenne Kid had negotiated the width of the street and now stood in the doorway of the carpenter shop. The din of the twin Colt's discharges left Hank Coffey with no real idea of the Kid's location. Carefully, he slipped his own gun around the edge of the counter. He fired. So did the Kid. Coffey howled and his pistol flew from his shattered right hand. The Kid walked into the store, grinning as he looked down at the hapless old lawman.

"Finish it, you little bastard."

"Get to your feet," the Kid replied.

"Go to hell," Coffey told him.

The Kid holstered his guns, walked over, grabbed Coffey by the lapels of his coat and heaved, hard, upward. The marshal winced as pain shot through his leg. Still, he swung at the Kid. The Kid fended off the blow, laughed and stepped back. He drew and kept his weapon levelled at Coffey. The Kid retrieved Coffey's gun, walked over and slipped it into the marshal's holster, then stepped back about ten paces and holstered his own gun.

"Now you sunuvabitch, pull on me."

"Kid, what the hell." The Kid's head jerked to the left, the sound of his brother's voice—outside. Hank Coffey went for his gun. As the hammer clicked into place and he levelled the weapon's barrel, he used his left hand to push away from the counter. He heard a shot, but he knew he hadn't fired yet. The Kid had. Hank Coffey pulled the trigger.

The Kid's bullet ripped into the old marshal's left side, tore through his rib cage and ripped into his left lung. Blood spewed from Hank's mouth, he gasped, choked, staggered and went down. His own shot hit the Cheyenne Kid in the belly, just above his belt buckle. He was so shocked he dropped his gun, grabbed at himself and looked down—just before he fell.

## Dean McElwain

Caleb Bullock still couldn't see Marshal Coffey. He did see his kid brother take a bullet in the gut and leaped from his horse. The man with him shouted, "We gotta high tail it out o' here." When he saw Caleb Bullock disappear into the carpenter's shop, he spurred his horse and the animal lurched forward. Just then, the figure of a man appeared at the corner of the building. The rider slapped at his waistband, reaching for the pistol. He cleared it from its holster just as the man at the corner raised, aimed and fired the old scatter gun. The discharge struck the man on the horse full in the chest. He flew backwards, landing on his shoulders and neck. His neck snapped but he didn't feel it. He was already dead. Nathan Hale Breed, New York newspaperman, had just killed his first man.

The Cheyenne Kid, known to some as Daniel Trent Bullock, died with tears in his eyes and the word "Momma" on his lips. Caleb Bullock might have looked closer at the old marshal and even finished him off had it not been for the discharge of a shotgun. Caleb darted outside, saw his friend in the street and turned to face the man at the corner. Suddenly, the man was jerked out of sight. In his place stood a much taller man. A man with dark, piercing eyes, full moustache, and dressed all in black.

"It's over Bullock," Preacher said. He pulled back the frock coat, revealing the silver star. Caleb Bullock drew and fired, but he was late. Way too late, as Preacher's bullet pierced his heart. Jack Omohundro mumbled something to himself in reaction to the bounty hunter's movements.

Nate Breed's story, "The Day the Bullock Gang Died," included a poignant description of a man's feelings and thoughts when he takes another's life.

# TRAIL OF DEATH

At least one man's thoughts and feelings—Nathan Breed's. It was a day North Platte would long remember.

# 10

The Honorable Colonel William Frederick Cody, resplendent in a white, tall crowned stetson, buckskins and knee high, black leather boots, was escorted to the Senate Office of William Allison of the state of Iowa.

"Colonel Cody," Allison said, standing, smiling and extending his hand, "how absolutely wonderful to see you again." Cody said nothing. He glanced back over his shoulder until Allison's aide closed the door. Allison felt foolish, leaning over his desk. He straightened up, slightly miffed at Cody's snub.

"I am not normally a man given to displays of temper or the use of profanity, sir," Cody said, "but you are a Goddam liar!"

"Colonel Cody. You can't . . ."

"Don't you *dare* to presume to tell me what I cannot do. I gave my word—my word of honor sir, to my Indian friends. You thrust a knife into my back. Worse, Senator, your blatant disregard for my report, to say nothing of a United States government treaty, has endangered the lives of every white citizen west of Omaha and north of Kansas."

Senator Allison, his face flushed, slumped into his chair. Cody continued harranguing the politician for several minutes. Finally, the rangy frontiersman leaned forward, resting his upper body on clenched fists against the Senator's desk top.

"I intend to seek an audience with the President," Cody said. "And I will use every means at my disposal to set this travesty straight. Why even my own friends on the trail will spit at the mention of my name." Cody straightened. "I will not be able to fault them. Count yourself fortunate, Senator. Had you done this to me in my own country—in my beloved west—I should have staked you out and left you for my blood brothers."

Buffalo Bill Cody's atypical actions had been prompted by his discovery of the army's expedition into the Black Hills. Cody, his meeting with the major chiefs already arranged, had been told by Senator Allison to cancel it. The plan for the Black Hills excursion had been scrapped and Cody was delighted. Allison even promised to inform Cody's friends so Cody could resume his plans to journey to Europe.

Allison lied. The authority in Washington had determined that they did not wish to risk rejection by the plains tribes. They would not ask. They would organize an even bigger expedition and launch it before the Indians could protest.

At the beginning of the Moon of Red Cherries, Star Chief Pahuska, the Long Hair, rode at the head of the Seventh Cavalry regiment out of Fort Abraham Lincoln, Dakota Territory.

Lieutenant-Colonel George Armstrong Custer commanded more than a thousand troopers and hundreds of civilian personnel who manned scores of canvas covered supply wagons. The blue and white snake slithered its way south, along the Missouri River to its confluence with the Cheyenne. By 15 July, a huge base camp was established near Buck Mountain—a northeast entryway into the Black Hills.

Prior to the summer of 1874, miners, trappers and hunters had teased, pawed and tormented the sovereign virginity of the sacred Paha Sapa. Now, the White man's phallus of greed was about to be inserted and the savage rape completed.

Jim Hickok rode point for the expedition. By appointment, Hickok was the chief of scouts. In loose terminology, this was true. He assigned certain tasks, appointed those who would ride drag or flank, and named both white and Indian scouts to accompany the geologists on the trek. The man who was the actual Chief of scouts was Lonesome Charley Reynolds.

Charlie knew the Paha Sapa better than any other white man. Probably better than many Indians. At one time or another, he had ridden into every corner of it. Lonesome Charley was a big, likeable and incredibly simple man. He spoke in words of one syllable for the most part, usually only when asked and he was almost never wrong in his intuitions about Indians. While Hickok might be as far as a half day away from the main body, Lonesome Charley would venture two and sometimes three days out.

Custer had engaged in only one official operation on which he was not accompanied by Lonesome Charley Reynolds. Many claimed the outcome

# TRAIL OF DEATH

would have been far different had Lonesome Charley been along that time. It was the attack on Black Kettle's Cheyenne down on the Washita in '68.

Jack Omohundro and Colorado Charlie Utter rode drag on the expedition's first leg. The three week trek from Fort Lincoln to the base of Buck Mountain had been negotiated in near perfect weather. Scattered among the white scouts were two Arikara, two Ree, a strikingly handsome Crow named Curley, and the mixed breed Sioux named Bloody Knife. Of the Indian scouts, Bloody Knife was Custer's most favored. Only Charley Reynolds' words carried more weight with the Seventh's commanding officer.

Custer ordered a full day's rest at the base camp, once it was established. His men were grateful. So were the scouts. On the afternoon of that day, Lieutenant-Colonel George Custer found himself suddenly in company he had not requested. Jim Hickok, J.D. Preacher, Charlie Utter, the expedition's offical reporter, a young man named Mark Kellogg and Preacher's last minute addition, Nathan Breed.

"Gentlemen," Custer said, smiling cordially. "I suggest to you that we move this pow wow out of the confines of this tent." Custer's younger brother, Tom, held the tent flaps while the first three men exited.

"They look a little hot around the collars, Autie," Tom said. Few people addressed Custer by his boyhood name. Tom did. So did Boston Custer and, on occasion where she felt bound to sway his thinking, so did Custer's wife, Libby. Only when Custer's nephew was present did everyone refrain from the name's use. The nephew's name was Autie Reed.

"Is Charley Reynolds back?" Tom shook his head. "Damn!" Custer emerged, smiling. "Now gentlemen, what seems to be the problem?"

"Could be a mighty big one," Jim Hickok said, "if'n this is right." He handed Custer a dispatch which had arrived only that morning from Fort Pierre. "Young Nate Breed's newspaper in New York telegraphed about it." Hickok looked at Breed. "Two weeks back mebbe." Breed nodded. Hickok continued with, "I had Kellogg here confirm it. This is the answer we got." Custer read.

> Colonel W. F. Cody was informed on 12 January to cease any further plans for seeking Indian permission to enter the Black Hills. The expedition was ordered cancelled. In fact, only Colonel Cody was so informed. This appears a deliberate distortion.

The dispatch was unsigned. Custer's brow was wrinkled into a deep frown. He glanced up once or twice but re-read the message several times. Finally, he held it up. "Who sent this?"

"My publisher," Mark Kellogg replied. "He did confirm it with the war department however. It seems the entire plan was formulated—or at least approved—by Senator Allison."

"Did you know of it?" Preacher asked. Custer eyed the lanky Tennessean. He didn't know J.D. Preacher as well as he knew Hickok or Reynolds, but he felt considerable respect for the man.

"I give you my solemn oath," Custer finally said, "that I, nor any of my officers, had so much as an inkling of this." He shook the paper, finally crushing it. "Damn! Those lying . . ." Tom Custer put his arm on his brother's shoulder. Tom's greatest fear for Autie was not his death at the hands of the Indians. Rather, George Custer's burning ambitions and hatred for the Washington bureaucrats, who lined their pockets at the expense of innocent people—even their own United States Army.

"If that's the fact," Preacher said, "we're in a tight." Custer looked up. He considered Preacher, then the others, and smiled, wistfully. "That's the fact, that's sure the fact. A spot? Not at all, Preacher. That's why those . . . *gentlemen* in Washington approved a larger and better equipped expedition. The Indians weren't looking for us, they're not prepared and we'll be through and gone before they could muster the strength to deal with this." He stretched his hand out and gestured to the base camp.

"Could they ever?" Tom asked.

"Oh no. Not if it were purely a military operation. Nothing the red man is capable of would stand against an entire regiment. This, well, this is more a Sunday stroll in the park. We could defend ourselves, but. . . ."

"When do we break camp and return to Fort Lincoln?" Breed asked. Preacher looked down and barely nodded his head in reaction to young Breed's naivete. He anticipated Custer's reply.

"Break camp? Go back?" Custer chuckled. "Your dispatch is valuable only to the extent that it confirms a story for you, Breed. I have an official order in *my* dispatch case. I am bound to carry it out. I've seen nothing to alter that." Breed's quick scan of the faces around him answered any further queries he might pose.

"Jim," Custer said to Hickok, "Charley Reynolds

is due back at anytime. When he gets here, I'd like you," Custer turned, "and you, Preacher and Charley, to join me for dinner." Hickok nodded.

As the group dispersed, Hickok and Preacher, tenting together, chatted about the turn of events.

"You believe 'im, Preacher man?" Hickok was looking down.

"I believe him, Jim. George Custer is a puzzlement to me in a lot of ways, but he's no liar."

"Yep, that's how I see it."

"There'll be hell to pay for this, and they won't be payin' back east."

"Uh huh. May be hell to pay yet today," Jim said, grinning, "when Lonesome Charley finds out."

Lonesome Charley Reynolds found out. He listened to Hickok explain what had happened. He heard Mark Kellogg tell about Cody's return to the plains in an effort to meet and appease the main tribal chiefs. His craggy face showed no change in expression as opinions were offered by Colorado Charlie Utter, Texas Jack Omohundro and some of the Indian scouts. The trio, Reynolds, Hickok and Preacher went to dinner.

Again, Lonesome Charley listened. He heard young Tom Custer's tone of bravado and his talk of the inevitability of white supremacy. Finally, Custer's Chief of Scouts listened to the Seventh's commander, the white man's hero of the Washita.

"In a hundred years," Custer said in summary, "school children will read a book about this expedition. If nothing else, it will teach them that the personal beliefs and principles of one man—or even many men—cannot dominate or deter progress." Custer smiled. He turned to Reynolds. "Charley, I don't recall you ever being so damned quiet."

# TRAIL OF DEATH

"You're wrong, Gen'rul." Charley Reynolds had never stopped addressing Custer by the officer's Civil War, brevet rank. That of Brigadier General. "Injuns won't blame Cody or Grant—none o' them fellas. They ain't forgot the Washita, Gen'rul. They won't forget this," he said, jabbing a finger toward the ground. He lifted it then and pointed it right at George Custer's nose. "An' they won't forget you, Pahuska." Charley took a long pull from a jug which almost never left his side. He swilled the liquid from cheek-to-cheek in his mouth and then swallowed. "They'll come fer ya, Custer." He shook his head. "I wish I knew where an' when, but you can count on it sure. They'll come fer ya."

Preacher's eyes shifted to Custer as Charley Reynolds made his prediction. He saw a surprised, almost shocked expression. Preacher glanced at the faces of the others. They too seemed stunned by quiet Lonesome Charley Reynolds' words. One of the most surprised, Custer's baby brother, Tom. He would relate later that he had never heard Charley Reynolds call Custer only by his last name. Charley's final words on the matter elicited even more shock, perhaps even some deep feelings of foreboding.

"Them young-uns you talked about, you be right," he said. "They'll be a book sure, an' they'll read it an' learn."

Charley took another pull on his jug, wiped his mouth and said, "But I don't think it'll say much about what we're doin' here. I think they'll be learnin' 'bout you, Gen'rul. You an' the red men."

"Charley," Preacher finally said, "I'm not saying you're wrong, but you seem to place a lot of stock in the connection between this expedition and the Indian's feelings about Mister Custer. I'm not sure I follow. I don't like this either, or the way it was done. Still," Preacher added, "I don't see a lot of difference between this and a lot of other injustices to the red man."

"They's not a lot, bounty hunter, they's jist one. A'fore now, we kil't the Injuns' body. Doubt that there's a creature livin' that's got a better understandin'—or a closer kinship with the Lord than an Injun. We don't understand 'im so we don't accept that but it's a fact just the same. Well sir, ridin' in here we're messin' with his spirit. We're threatenin' to kill the Wakan Tanka—the Injun's God. He'll be a mite riled."

The dinner party broke up. Even Tom Custer found himself suddenly very tired. George Custer asked Preacher to stay behind for a few minutes.

"Preacher, I don't drink. Never have. I know you enjoy an occasional whiskey. Most men who do drink don't do it around me." Custer smiled. "Except for Charley Reynolds. He does as he damn pleases mostly. Anyway, I don't mind. If you'd like a drink, have one."

"I'm grateful," Preacher said, "but I only drink one brand and it's in short supply. I'll pass." Custer nodded. "What's on your mind, Colonel?"

Custer considered Preacher and his question. He stroked the droopy moustache for a few moments and then he looked the Widow Maker right in the eye.

"I don't know you too well Preacher, or you me. A lot of the men who were here tonight either won't speak their mind, or they won't say anything at all. I'd like your honest opinion of this expedtion, Charley Reynold's prediction, and of me. Will you give it?"

"If I can give it with the understanding that it's

# TRAIL OF DEATH

open to change, Colonel. As you've said, we don't know each other that well." Custer nodded. "I think this expedition should never have happened, permission from the Indians or not. I thought that before tonight, but not for all the right reasons. Charley Reynolds cleared some of those up for me, and he strengthened all of them."

"But you're a realist, Preacher. You must know that if we—the Seventh Cavalry—hadn't done it, someone else would have."

"I know, and I hope when it's over, some here will argue that whatever we find is shared with the Indians. If it had to be done, I'd rather see the men now doing it involved than anyone else."

"And Charley's prediction?"

"Given what I know, what I've read, and what I've heard, yeah," Preacher said, "I think he's right. I'm not certain just what he's really thinking will happen, but I think he's right."

"And *me*, Preacher? What about me?"

"You're a little too ambitious for the wrong things, I think. You're a man who could accomplish a great deal for this country, and at a crucial time in her history." Preacher smiled. "I think it was that English gent, Shakespeare, who said something about the whole world being a stage and we're just actors."

"You think of me as an actor?"

"Yes sir, in a way, and pretty miscast."

"What should I be, Preacher?" Custer leaned back unbuttoning his tunic, then took a deep breath and added, smiling, "President?"

"That who you want to be, Colonel?" Custer felt a twinge in his belly at the question. Was Preacher speaking acidly? Custer wasn't sure.

"I could serve many if I was."

"Or none."

Custer smiled. "You're a damned perceptive gent for no older than you are. Just how old is that?"

"Twenty eight."

"How would you have me serve, Preacher?"

Preacher sighed. "Well Colonel, if the Indians come to hate you as much as Charley Reynolds thinks they will, then I figure you could gain an equal amount of respect. Maybe that book you both talked about would relate to the youngsters how a fellow named George Custer helped to open the west and blend two civilizations together in one land."

"A lofty goal," Custer said, rubbing his chin and smiling. "A lofty goal indeed." He looked up. "You didn't like me much down on the Washita, did you?"

"I didn't like what you did, but I didn't have all the facts. I didn't know how accurate your scouting reports were. I . . ." Custer cut him short with a hand held high.

"I make decisions, Preacher—for right or for wrong, I make them. I don't back off after I do, and I don't apologize for them. So the record is straight between us. I knew. I knew everything."

"You slaughtered old women and children, Custer. You're a hero for it. There had to be a better way."

Custer reached behind him, produced a dispatch case and removed from it a thick sheaf of papers. "Glance through them, Preacher."

Preacher did. They related Indian attacks on wagon trains, homesteads, railroad workers, telegraph workers, stagecoaches, even small settlements. The atrocities perpetrated included live scalping, unspeakable mutilations, torture, kidnapping and burning alive. Preacher returned the papers.

# TRAIL OF DEATH

"There wasn't a better way," Custer said.

"You've asked me for opinions, now give me one. How do you feel about the Indian? Not as a soldier, but as a human being?"

"If I were an Indian," Custer replied thoughtfully, "I would greatly prefer to cast my lot among those of my people who adhered to the free open plains rather than submit to the confined limits of a reservation."

Two more wagons arrived on the following morning. Preacher learned that they had come at Custer's personal request. They were full of newspaper reporters. After having given permission for Breed to accompany the expedition, Custer decided it should be wide open. Preacher winced upon learning of the arrival, and the reason.

Autie Custer was among the first outside to greet the members of the press. Among them was Samuel Barrows of the New York *Tribune* and a fanciful, rotund little fellow named Ed Judson. The latter displayed almost as much interest in the scouts with the expedition as he did the country itself. He had already written about some of them under the pen name, Ned Buntline.

By noon, the winding column was ready to move into the very heart of the Paha Sapa. The day's march would end at the spot selected by the party's chief engineer, William Ludlow. It was a beautiful valley, nestled between the highest of the area's peaks. It was named French Creek.

Preacher rode to the head of the column with Custer himself. Nearly all of the Indian scouts were there, as was Charley Reynolds. Charley turned his horse and faced the Seventh cavalry's buckskin clad commander. "Turn back, Gen'rul. This'll bring ya more grief than you need."

Custer smiled. "I can't do that, Charley."

"Didn't figger you would. Some o' the Arikaras won't ride in."

"Put them on relay riding back to Fort Lincoln. I have mail, so have the men, and the reporters will have dispatches. They will serve us best in that capacity." Custer stood up in his stirrups, looked back over the lengthy column and smiled. Preacher knew he was in his element. Perhaps, Preacher thought, the only change Custer would feel noteworthy at that point would be if he was leading an attack! "You'll be with me, won't you Charley," Custer asked when he turned back.

Charley Reynolds removed his hat, displaying a considerably retarded hair line. "Sure, Gen'rul," he replied, grinning. "I got nothin' to lose."

Preacher was reminded of a campaign or two during the war at the French Creek camp that night. Fires danced their flickering displays in front of each of the tents. The odor of burning wood mingled with that of roasting venison and strong coffee. The strains of mouth harps and concertinas floated on the night air, broken occasionally by off-key singing attempts and accolades of laughter.

Preacher sat before his own tent, enjoying his pipe and savoring the taste and texture of a glass of *Teton Jack*. Smoke from the campfires went almost straight up until it drew even with the tops of surrounding peaks. The smoke appeared to be woven around hemp rope until the high winds caught it. The night was peaceful, nature was peaceful, only men, Preacher thought, were not at peace with each other.

"Evening, Preacher." The lanky bounty man looked up to see Nate Breed. "Mind if I join you?"

"Sit."

"The Black Hills express got underway tonight," Nate said. Preacher looked quizzical. "Custer's Indian scouts. They're riding in relays back to Fort Lincoln. The Lieutenant's brother dubbed it the Black Hills express."

"Did you use it?"

"Not yet. I haven't quite figured what to write, what to say." Breed shrugged. "Mostly, I don't know how to say it. Even Barrows," Nate said and then emphasized, "and he's as good as they come, even *he's* having trouble. Look here, Preacher. Look what he wrote."

> An Eden in the clouds—how shall I describe it! I might as well try to paint the flavor of a peach or the odor of a rose.

"I'd say that's a fair effort," Preacher said. "The place defies description." Preacher sucked on his pipe but it was out. He fished for a match and Breed provided one. It also gave the youthful reporter an opening.

"You must have had quite a talk with Custer last night." Preacher blew smoke and looked at Breed. He said nothing. "Did you talk about the expedition?"

"Not sure that conversation should leave the Colonel's tent."

"I can ask him."

"Good idea."

"How come you're so bitter, Preacher? I mean . . . well . . . I know some of the story. I know what happened in Tennessee, and who did it and what you did. I'd guess what happened to you and yours happened to lots o' folks."

"And they're not bitter?"

"Maybe they are, they just don't make a profession of it."

"And you think I'm bitter? That's your word Breed, not mine."

"Then give me *your* word."

"I'm a professional killer."

"I don't believe that."

"You're a hard man, Breed. Nothing satisfies you. You tell me you want my side of the story and when I give it, you don't believe it."

"Killing is what you do Preacher, it's not what you are." Preacher thought back to a gun drummer he'd met once. The drummer had said something similar. "How do you see yourself?"

"Realistically," Preacher replied. "I am what I am, I do what I do, and neither your words or mine make a damned bit of difference."

"But you're here. There are no bounties here, no fast gun hands or bank robbers or murderers. And you've done this kind of thing before. That's the man I want to learn about. The *real* J.D. Preacher."

"I rode to the Washita because a friend asked me to. I'm here for the same reason."

"It's that simple, is it?"

"Just that simple," Preacher said. He reached into his vest pocket, withdrew a newspaper clipping and handed it to Breed. "Read what is circled, Breed. Read that and you'll know how I feel about what I'm doing here, and to some degree about the men who asked me to be here."

Breed opened it and found he was staring at a printed copy of the treaty signed with the plains Indians in 1868. He scanned it until he found the words which had been circled by Preacher.

> No white person or persons shall be permitted to settle upon or occupy any portion of the territory, or without the consent of the Indians pass through the same.

"If you read ahead of that Breed, that is if you don't already know it, you'll find that was written about this country, about the Black Hills."

"Alright Preacher," Breed said, handing back the article, "you've given me a little insight into what you feel. Now show me something different than I get from other men. Show me some answers to the problems, some solutions to go along with those lofty feelings."

"A pair of matched pistols won't do it, Breed. Not mine, not Jim Hickok's. A legend like Bill Cody or George Custer won't do it." Preacher turned, pushed himself up until he was sitting Indian style and looked, hard, at young Nathan Hale Breed. "*You* Breed, you and men like you. You're the answer. Write it down, bring it to the attention of the public. Let them bring it to the attention of the men in Washington. Make so much smoke that they'll have to send somebody to put out the fire. You reporters are full of questions, that's sure. Some of 'em most probably, are good questions. Justified. The only damned problem I see with you is that you always ask them of the wrong people." Preacher got up, picked up his flask of whiskey, tapped the tobacco out of his pipe on the bottom of it and then said, "Good night, Mister Breed."

# 11

The buffalo grass had turned brown and it was now the first days of the season the Indians call the Moon of the Falling Leaves. Jim Hickok had collected his pay, hurrahed Bismarck and ridden off with Charlie Utter. Texas Jack Omohundro followed suit, planning, he said, to romance his favorite girl through the winter. His favorite girl was Texas!

Most of the Indian scouts remained at Fort Lincoln, and Lonesome Charley Reynolds remained on the payroll as their chief. Now, in early September, J.D. Preacher readied himself to ride out. He would journey to Cheyenne first and there try to pick up word of Brock Sturgis and Mexican Joe Juniper. He knew there would be a brand new list of *Wanteds* as well.

"Door's open," he said, in response to a light rapping at his barrack's door. It opened slowly, Preacher squinted and somewhat tensed.

"It's Libby Custer, Mister Preacher." He smiled.

She was the first person, male or female, who had resisted all his efforts to stop her from using the word Mister in front of his name.

"Come in, ma'am." She did, leaving the door slightly ajar. "Everything alright?"

"It will be," she said, "if I am successful in my imminent imposition upon you, Mister Preacher. I have received some most exciting news today and I would like to host a small party in honor of Beau . . . uh," she smiled, "of my husband."

"I see," Preacher said, "but how can I help you?"

"By being there," Libby Custer replied. "Autie spoke very highly of you. He puts on you the same esteem as Jim Hickok. I'd like the opportunity to test his judgment." She was smiling. The remark was in jest. Preacher liked this woman, though he'd met her only briefly, and they had spent only short times together—all of them somewhat stiff and formal.

"I'm honored," Preacher said, never one to pass on a winning hand. "But I would agree only on one condition. It is, perhaps, too demanding of me." He could see Mrs. Custer's surprise and disappointment.

"Is it a condition which . . . well, which I could meet?"

"It is," Preacher said.

"Then I shall try, sir."

"You must stop calling me sir and mister. I prefer Preacher, and that, ma'am, is my condition." Preacher smiled.

"I'm sorry," she said, "it is absolutely out of the question. Far too presumptuous of you, and I should imagine that you are quite ashamed of yourself for even suggesting such familiarity." Her tone was firm, her small, round face beaming. The corners of her mouth began a slow curl upwards. A moment later, Libby Custer and J.D. Preacher were both laughing. In Preacher's case, it had been a very long time since he had last laughed.

The occasion for the party had come from Washington, through General Terry at the Department of the Missouri. It was official confirmation of Lieutenant-Colonel Custer's promotion, by field brevet, back to his rank of Brigadier General. He was also named commanding officer of Fort Abraham Lincoln.

"Congratulations General," Preacher said. "That gold you found in the Black Hills wears well on your shoulders."

"A two edged knife, Preacher," Custer said, grinning, "you wield a two edged knife." Custer twisted his neck until he could get a look at the epaulet on his left shoulder. "I must agree however that gold does become me." Libby Custer approached.

"Good evening," Preacher said, hesitating, glancing at Custer and then smiling and adding, "Libby."

She returned the smile, almost a chuckle. "Preacher," she said, "you look quite striking this evening." Preacher's eyes shifted to Custer's face. His was a stern countenance and he frowned as he glanced at his wife. He removed a glove, the standard cavalry issue, yellow gauntlet. Preacher was about to receive another lesson from Autie Custer.

"Libby told me everything," he said and slapped the gauntlet along the side of his leg. He was laughing. "Come Preacher, meet some of my new staff arrivals." Preacher nodded. He was shaking his head at the exchanges of humor between them,

# TRAIL OF DEATH

in which he had come out the loser in all cases. The Custers reminded him of home, of Bradburn Hill and another time.

By eight o'clock, most of the guests had arrived. Talk of the expedition into the Black Hills had ended and the orchestra, in fact a section of the Seventh's band, began to play. Preacher found an isolated corner. Minutes later, Libby Custer found him.

"Tell me about yourself, Preacher."

"There isn't much to tell," he said.

"I have heard there is a great deal, but that you simply refuse to discuss it."

"Nate Breed must have talked to you."

She smiled. "Young Mister Breed is, indeed, a firebrand. He seems determined to report stories about you and Jim Hickok and others like you. I'll not press the issue."

"I'm grateful," Preacher said.

"Do you think my husband egotistical?" Preacher turned his head and looked into Libby Custer's eyes. Now, she was serious.

"That's too strong a term."

"Ambitious is what I believe he told me you said."

"It was."

"Is that wrong?"

"Not at all, but in this country it can lead to faulty judgment."

"And that means death out here, doesn't it, Preacher?"

He considered her and admired her forthright approach. She was a woman of substance, wise beyond her years. In fact, Libby Custer was only four years older than J.D. Preacher.

"It could," he said.

"Do you think Autie would make a good President? He's been approached, you know?"

"I don't know much about Presidents, Libby—good or bad."

"He is a leader."

"That he is."

"You think he'd be wasted in Washington, don't you?"

"Yes, I do. He knows the Indians. He has their respect."

"Their hatred I'd think."

"Hatred is a powerful emotion, Libby. It presents a challenge to those who harbor it for someone. I doubt that any man would challenge something, or someone, that he doesn't respect."

"You're an amazing man, Preacher, truly amazing. I've heard stories—Jim Hickok mostly, about your almost magical skill with pistols. Surely it cannot rival your intellect and your philosophy."

The conversation was as heavy as a velvet curtain and Preacher was not comfortable with it. He smiled, "I've never really put that premise to the test," he said. "Most of the men I face would shoot me several times while I was trying."

There was a commotion at the door. Libby looked up and so did Preacher. Libby smiled. "Ah . . . at last," she said. She took Preacher's arm, stood up and he followed, frowning. She led him across the dance floor and the officers parted upon seeing her approach. Preacher found himself face-to-face with one of the most beautiful women he'd ever seen.

"Libby! Dear, dear Libby! How wonderful to see you." The girl hugged Libby Custer, then they parted.

"Preacher," Libby said, "I want you to meet Shannon MacKenzie." She turned to the girl. "Shannon, please make the acquaintance of Mister J.D. Preacher of Tennessee. He has been serving with Jim Hickok and Charley Reynolds on Autie's scout staff."

Preacher's eyes met those of Shannon MacKenzie and he felt a warmth—no, a burning—in the pit of his stomach, then it crawled into his groin. He licked his lips, remembered something a gambler had told him once and hoped like hell Shannon MacKenzie couldn't read his mind.

"My pleasure, uh . . ." he glanced at Libby. She smiled and let him squirm a bit.

"It is *Miss* MacKenzie," Libby finally said.

"I'm pleased to meet you, Mister Preacher." Shannon curtsied.

Libby Custer said, "This will never do, not at all." She looked at Shannon and added, "This stubborn man will not allow himself to be addressed by any name save his last one—Preacher. That and that alone."

"I'm called Shannon, Preacher." She smiled.

"Now, you two are wasting time. You can visit while you dance." Preacher hadn't danced since the war. A party in a Virginia home one evening, after a particularly successful raid by Mosby's Rangers. He looked at Libby Custer. Clearly, she was playing at cupid here and Preacher's face felt warm from the guilt of his continuing thoughts about Shannon MacKenzie.

"May I?" he said. Shannon nodded as they walked off, Libby Custer smiled—a smile of satisfaction.

Preacher was smitten. He was lusting for

Shannon MacKenzie, in his mind, but at the same time, he was angry, elated and confused. Deep inside, J.D. Preacher of Bradburn Hill, Tennessee, was probably frightened. He was up against something which could not be settled with a fast draw.

At night, he retired with visions of Shannon foremost in his thoughts. Perhaps the most beneficial result of it was the fact that, at last, all visions of horror and the faces of Rosamond Langehorn and his sister had been obliterated.

Preacher changed his plans. He signed on with Charley Reynolds as a scout. Once again, Brock Sturgis and Joe Juniper were forgotten. Preacher actually began to have thoughts of a normal life again. He could hang up the matching pistols and settle down. He knew he would have a job with the army.

Fall faded away. The scouts rode in and out of Fort Lincoln with alarming news. No Indians were to be found, save those who had become reservation Indians. By the time of the Moon When the Deer Shed Their Horns—just days before Christmas, 1874—General Custer called a meeting of his top scouts and officers' staff.

"I have been relieved of command," he said. Most of those present, regular army personnel, were already aware of the fact. Those who were not, were simply too stunned to even respond. "As some of you are aware, I have never been a favorite of the President." Custer smiled but it belied the look in his eyes and the increasing visibility of dark circles under them.

"Even during the war," Custer continued, "Grant refused to acknowledge my accomplishments. He once told General Sherman that I was not worthy to polish his boots." Custer's voice grew faint. "My God," he muttered. He fell silent. Suddenly, his head jerked upwards. "I will not yield without a fight. I am returning to Washngton and, by Godfrey, when I come home, back to the west, I will be in command of the Seventh."

"Here, here," some of the officers shouted. Captain Keough raised his hat and launched into a trio of "Hip-Hip Hurrahs." Custer issued his last official orders, another scouting foray into the Black Hills, and then dismissed the men. He asked that Preacher remain behind.

"General," Preacher said, when the last of the staff had departed, "I've never been to Washington, but I've seen their damned commissions and read their treaties and heard their promises. Get some help. What you're about to face will be a hundred-fold worse than anything the Sioux or Cheyenne will ever throw at you."

"I may be all finished," Custer said. "Libby is going with me. I'd hoped she would," he smiled, "although I tried to talk her out of it. I don't think she ever believed me."

"You can be sure of that, General. Libby can't be fooled."

"She's taking this hard. Too hard. I've seen the fear in her eyes when I've ridden into a campaign. This is worse. She asked me to convey her best to you, and hoped you would look after young Shannon."

"Tell her not to worry," Preacher said.

"There is something else, Preacher." Custer handed Preacher a folder. "I suppose you've read the accounts in the newspapers about the results of our expedition." Preacher nodded. Then, he looked up and frowned. "They are, well—understated."

"The gold finds are larger?"

"Much larger," Custer said. Suddenly, he was smiling the smile Preacher recognized when Custer was pleased with himself. "That discovery is my hole card Preacher, my ace. There is more gold in the Black Hills than anyone can imagine. By spring there will be camps all over it. By summer, communities." Custer got to his feet and walked around his desk. "Those mealy mouthed lackeys of Grant's won't be able to dispute that," he said, jabbing the folder with his index finger.

Preacher glanced through it. The official engineering reports were staggering. The gold and silver ore was some of the best grade ever discovered west of the Mississippi. Preacher closed the folder, handed it back and shook his head. Custer thought it to be a gesture of disbelief.

"Do you realize what this means?" Custer said. "Do you comprehend the enormity of it? I've cut a road into the Black Hills, my friend," he reached out and slapped Preacher on the shoulder, "and now I'm about to see it paved with gold."

"What you *cut*," Preacher said, his tone caustic, "is the heart from Wakan Tanka. You violated the sacred Paha Sapa. I knew you had to obey your orders, Custer, but I didn't think you'd use the results to save your own hide."

"Don't go moral on me, Preacher. I'm a survivor—the same as you are." He thrust the report toward Preacher's face. "And *this* is my weapon." He turned on his heel and walked back around his desk. He tossed the report down and then looked up. "I may ride into Washington on a

muddy trail, but I'll ride back on a street of gold."
"That golden road, General, will be covered with blood. In a year it will be the trail of death!"

# 12

The Seventh Cavalry's scouts spent the first three months of 1875 outside the walls of Fort Lincoln. They rode to every known winter camp site used by the Sioux and the other plains tribes. They found no Indians.

In mid April, Charley Reynolds left Preacher in charge and rode south into Nebraska, and down to the Republican River Valley. There, he met with Red Cloud. They were old friends, but that fact didn't help. Charley learned nothing—at least directly. Red Cloud's refusal to discuss the whereabouts of those who now led the warring factions among the tribes, told Charley Reynolds much more than he cared to know.

By May he was back at Fort Lincoln and the Seventh was getting ready to move out. Charley met with Preacher.

"We found them Injuns what's been missin' all winter." Preacher nodded. "Last report puts more'n

# TRAIL OF DEATH

a hunnert miners kil't up in the Black Hills."

"And it isn't Red Cloud, is it Charley?"

Charley Reynolds shook his head. "Sioux got themselves a medicine man—Sittin' Bull—an' the meanest redskin what ever set a horse, Crazy Horse."

"Charley, did you talk to Bloody Knife yet?"

Charley looked puzzled. "Nope."

"You'd better. He and I found a camp—big—four or five weeks back. Down along Wounded Knee creek."

"What bunch?"

"That's just it, Charley, they were all mixed in. Sioux, Cheyenne, Black Foot. Hell, Bloody Knife said he even saw signs of Nez Perce."

"Nez Perce! Them's goddam Idaho injuns. Never heer'd o' them liftin' a finger against a white man."

"Renegades, Bloody Knife called them."

Lonesome Charley Reynolds fished in a pocket for a cigar. He bit off the end, lit the cigar, puffed on it in short breaths and then said, "The bastards are makin' peace 'tween one another. That's how's come we didn't find none of 'em last winter."

"General Terry is due here any day. I'd assumed the Seventh was moving into the hills to protect the miners. Is there more to it than that?"

"That's the standin' orders, Preacher," Charley said, "but they'd better scrap 'em. We don't stop them hostiles from gittin' together, it'll take a damn heap more bluecoats than we got here to round 'em up." Charley looked at Preacher now, a half smile on his face. "Custer ain't doin' too well either, is he?"

"He's in a tight."

"An' you? You quittin' me?"

"I am."

"That there spit of a girl melted down them gun

barrels, did she?" Charley was grinning. Preacher nodded. "She gonna hog tie you?"

"I haven't asked her yet, if that's what you mean."

Charley Reynolds laughed. "Hell son, that there askin' is just a formality. Woman gits a bead on ya once't, don't make no difference if'n you ask or not, yore a goner."

"I'm meeting her in Bismarck this afternoon, Charley. No one else knows. I'd appreciate it if they didn't, 'til she gets back."

"Back?"

"She's taking the stage south to Fort Pierre and a river packet down to Omaha to get her sister. We'll be married when they return." Preacher pointed. "Here, I hope. You're invited."

"Wouldn't miss it on a bet, Preacher. Been itchin' to see somebody what could outdraw you." Preacher laughed. "You sure you can hang them guns up, son? I mean, will the kind you went chasin' after let you?"

"I never thought so before, Charley," Preacher said, his voice much softer in tone than Charley had heard before, "but I never thought a lot of things before I met Shannon MacKenzie. I'll quit."

"Good luck to you then," Charley said. The two men shook hands warmly.

"Keep what hair you got left Charley."

"Damn sure intend to try," he said, frowning and then adding, "but I'd rather be ridin' into this with the Gen'rul."

Shannon MacKenzie was 22. Her face and features were almost angelic. Her neck long and slim, her breasts small but firm. She had chestnut brown hair with just the slightest trace of copper in

# TRAIL OF DEATH

it. It glistened in the right light. Her eyes were dark, inviting, her lips full and sensuous even when she didn't intend to display such feelings. She had come to display them often to J.D. Preacher.

At Edna Millington's boarding house in Bismarck, Preacher found Shannon packed and ready to leave. She was clad only in a dressing gown. After he entered her room, Shannon bolted the door and turned around.

"You've always been a gentleman to me, Preacher, and I've been the lady I'd hoped you'd fall in love with. Did you?"

"I did. I want to marry you Shannon, as soon as you get back."

"And I want to marry you," she replied, "but I want more than the words to take with me." She slipped out of the gown and Preacher's eyes saw, for the first time, what his mind had been trying to imagine for months. His thoughts had cheated him.

Shannon walked to him. They kissed. It was a long, deep, lust-filled kiss. Their tongues entwined and sought out the depths of each other's mouths. A strand of saliva glistened for a moment when they parted. Shannon undressed Preacher—slowly, deliberately. She teased him, while building upon her own desires.

Slowly, she pulled him toward the bed. She sat down on its edge, laid back and he knelt between her spread thighs. Immediately, Shannon tensed. J.D. Preacher would be her first man. He raised up, looked into her face and said, "I'll be gentle, very gentle." She closed her eyes.

Preacher's lips and tongue began nibbling and licking—teasing at Shannon's bare flesh. He slipped his big hands along her sides, his fingers tracing light paths toward her breasts. He found them, stroked them gently and kneaded their soft, plump forms. As he continued making love to her with his mouth, Preacher's thumbs and forefingers found Shannon's nipples. He squeezed and stroked them until they were hard little nubs of passion. He raised up, leaned over her and let his tongue explore their hardness. Shannon writhed with the passion of the sensations which shot through her body like little fires.

Unable to restrain herself any longer, she pulled Preacher's face to her own. She kissed him as he eased his huge frame atop hers and, together, they pushed themselves onto the full surface of the bed.

"Love me," she whispered, "love me on the inside." Preacher fed his blood-gorged shaft into her. He moved cautiously, easing the huge rod into the tightness of Shannon's vagina. She tensed, wincing with the first signals of pain. As the head of his tool reached her hymen, he stopped.

"There will be a moment of pain Shannon, just a few seconds." He kissed her ear, raised up and their eyes locked on one another. She nodded, almost imperceptibly. Preacher, bracing himself with his elbows and hands, eased forward. Shannon's mouth opened—wider, wider, and Preacher pushed—harder, harder. She cried out, the pressure was gone. She whined as he pushed against her, stroking now, slowly. He could feel the warmth of her juices mingled with the traces of blood which signified Shannon's emergence into womanhood.

No pain remained to Shannon, only a slight burning which was soon lost in the waves of pleasure which swept through every nerve in her body.

"Oh, Preacher ... my love ... my own. God ... oh. I never imagined ... oooh." She thrust against him, the fire building toward the inevitable explosion. Preacher continued pumping, moving his hands only so that he might again caress her breasts.

"I love you . . . God . . . how I love you," he said. The words slammed into his ears as though he'd been struck. Even in the passion of the moment Preacher could scarcely believe he'd spoken them.

Preacher and Shannon came together, suddenly, in a final impact of raw lust. Preacher's sperm surged forth in sporadic streams which seemed to fill every inch of available space. The warmth and moistness inside her was exhilarating to Shannon, and it increased her own final moment of joy. Bodies tensed, stiffened, held suspended for a moment, and then they fell, limp, in a beautiful exhaustion.

May was gone, June behind it. July seemed to crawl to a dead stop in the stifling heat of the great plains. At Shannon MacKenzie's pleadings, Preacher had stopped his scouting duties and turned to dispatch riding—eastbound—for the army. There were no Indians. Saloons, still untamed frontier towns and lawless settlements forced him to defend himself through the period, but he was no longer the Widow Maker. The bounty killer's instinct was in remission.

Nate Breed, so bent on making him a dime novel hero, gave up on J.D. Preacher. Now he followed the trails of men like Hickok, Charlie Utter, Jack Omohundro and some emerging gun men, both lawful and lawless, that the ever increasing wave of western expansion was introducing.

Preacher no longer stayed at Fort Lincoln. He rode there only to pick up a new dispatch or return one from one of the half-dozen or more forts to which he rode. He had purchased a small, white frame home on the north edge of Bismarck. It was cozy, and was one about which Shannon had often spoken. It had been occupied, but Preacher finally made an offer which brought results. Now, he could barely wait to see Shannon's reaction.

He had followed with interest and concern, George Custer's confrontation with the Washington hierarchy. Now, the Civil War's boy general and late hero of the Washita was in deep trouble. Indeed, he was credited with the opening of the Black Hills, but there were sharply divided factions even on that issue. Custer's friends had dwindled, his supporters all but vanished.

He would have known far less than he did save for the letters from Libby. She was, of course, delighted to learn of the forthcoming wedding. Preacher knew it pained Libby that she would probably not be present. She admonished Preacher never to reveal to Autie the contents of the letters she wrote.

In one, Libby revealed that they were so strapped for funds that they were living in a second rate boarding house. She wrote,

> . . . and we have seen Lawrence Barrett's performance of Julius Caesar nearly forty times. He is so good. We are given free admission.

Preacher returned to the small house on the evening of July 26. He still marveled at the fact that he had hung up his black mourning clothes as well as his guns. He ventured to town almost daily. At first, he'd been apprehensive—even nervous. Now, he was well known in Bismarck, as were his plans.

He had dined at the Lincoln Hotel dining room, picked up a copy of the Bismarck *Tribune,* chatted

# TRAIL OF DEATH

Down at the Lucky Lady, the barkeep informed Preacher the coffee was almost done. "Good. I'll need a cup when I get back."

"Back?"

"If I don't go to meet them, they'll be here and shoot up your place." He slipped on his coat, picked up the mare's leg and stepped outside. He'd reached the end of the boardwalk between the saloon and the general store when the trio of men stepped out of the Griswolds' place. Preacher stepped into the shadows.

The men cut across the street and walked down the opposite side. They were not taking any chances that this bounty hunter might have friends with him. They drew parallel to Preacher's position and passed it. They were about midway between his position and the front of the Lucky Lady. They stepped back into the street. Preacher stepped out of the shadows some forty feet from them.

"Gentlemen," he said. Heads jerked. Preacher fired, levered, fired, levered and fired again. All three shots, heavy calibre, struck high center in the men's chests—the sternum or breast bone. All three were dead before they struck the snow.

Preacher reached into the depths of his pocket, extracted three shells, reloaded the mare's leg, levered a shell into the chamber and walked toward the Three Brothers' saloon. The window was covered with a combination of steam and frost. He could not see inside. He opened the door, stepped in, raised the mare's leg and systematically destroyed the entire back bar—mirror, heavy oil painting of a nude woman and all the glassware.

"Give me the name of the third Griswold," he said. He glanced around the room. No one moved and no one spoke. One man's hand was very near the butt of his pistol. Preacher reckoned that the man was trying to determine just how many shots were left in whatever weapon Preacher was holding. He'd fired seven.

The barkeep finally managed a response. "Harry's 'is name. He ain't here. Rode to Cheyenne."

"There were five men who held up the Bismarck-Pierre stage last July. The Griswold boys were three of them, who were the other two?"

"Mister . . . I swear on my mother's grave, I don't know. If I knew I'd sure as hell tell you."

Preacher looked around the room. "Somebody knows. Who wants to volunteer."

"You're wrong about the Griswold boys. They didn't rob no stage." It was the man who'd been considering his chances against Preacher. Now, he stepped out of the corner. "They got their money from minin' mister, up in the Black Hills."

"Griswold keep an office here, barkeep?" The barkeep nodded in response to Preacher's question and pointed to a door at the far end of the bar. Preacher started toward it. His ears, even more sensitive as a result of his scouting experience, picked up the familiar, though faint, sound of metal against leather.

Preacher took three more steps, dropped to one knee, did a half twist and fired a last bullet from the mare's leg. It went through the head of the man who'd spoken moments before. Preacher worked the weapon's lever one more time but then shifted it to his left hand. No one else challenged him however.

In the saloon's office, after rifling through almost everything, Preacher found what he wanted. It was the U.S. army quartermaster's voucher for the denomination breakdowns and the total of payroll money to be carried by Wells-Fargo. At the top was

# TRAIL OF DEATH

the stamp of the Wells-Fargo company.

> U.S. Army Payroll
> for
> Fort Abraham Lincoln
> Bismarck DT
>
> Transport:
> Passenger Stage
> Bismarck-Pierre

The authorization signature, that of the agent Preacher killed in Pierre, didn't surprise him. What did was the driver's name. He had to sign for the shipment when it was loaded and would have had to do so again when it was delivered. Naturally, it hadn't reached its destination. The driver had been a substitute. Preacher knew, personally, the regular driver. He looked at the name again. *B. Sturgis*.

Preacher exited the Three Brothers' Saloon and within half an hour had exited the bustling community of Chugwater. He rode south, toward Cheyenne.

# 14

John H. Upton had been appointed as city marshal in Cheyenne on the second day of January, 1876. By mid-month, the man everyone now called Jack Henry, had rendered the lawless element in Cheyenne almost impotent.

Jack Henry stood nearly six and a half feet tall and weighed, give or take 15 pounds either way, about 300 pounds. He could be seen, day or night, on the streets of the Sodom of the Plains, carrying an axe handle in his left hand. On his right hip, he toted a Colt .45 Peacemaker and on a belt holster, waist level on his left side, a .44 calibre, 5 shot Remington.

By January 20, Jack Henry, a brand new jail at his disposal, had three of the six cells filled. In one of them reposed Mexican Joe Juniper. Jack Henry was very much aware of the threats made by Juniper's friends. All of the talk alluded to a break-out attempt. Jack Henry ignored the talk, took no additional precautions and steadfastly refused to

# TRAIL OF DEATH

change his daily routine.

South of Cheyenne, down along Lodgepole creek, Harry Griswold, Brock Sturgis, a pock-faced gun slinger called Laredo, and four out of work cow punchers camped and waited. The man they were waiting for was the circuit riding judge, H.G. Pettybone. When he arrived, the first case on his docket was Joe Juniper's. When Mexican Joe was transferred from his jail cell to the courthouse, the gang planned to make their move.

At least two men had ridden into Cheyenne from Chugwater during those weeks. Their purpose had been to warn Griswold and Sturgis about the bounty hunter who was closing on them fast. Unfortunately, they had done so admirable a job of staying out of sight, neither man had found them. Likewise, their pursuer had slipped into obscurity.

J.D. Preacher commandeered a vacant line shack just to the north of Cheyenne. There, he had lived and made his plans. He had purchased most of his needs by way of a nearby farmer with whom he had become acquainted. All 'round, what with Jack Henry's knowledge that at some point a breakout attempt would be made, the players had been dormant.

Daily, Preacher did venture far enough into Cheyenne to pick up a newspaper. He did so on the fourth day of February, 1876. The first story which caught his eye, also brought back distant memories and very current pain.

Washington 3 Febr. 1876
By direct order of President U.S. Grant, General Alfred Terry will organize the most ambitious campaign against the hostile Indians yet.

While the details of the effort weren't developed, General Terry said his own base of operations will be Fort Lincoln, Dakota Territory.

The announcement gave rise to speculation that the famed Civil War General and hero of the Washita, G.A. Custer, would be reinstated to active service.

Preacher read the article a second time and then turned to the column which, each day, reported territorial legal activities. Paydirt!

DOCKET—First Circuit Cheyenne WT
5 February 1876—H.G. Pettybone, Judge.

Territory vs. J. Juniper, alias, J.J. Hotchkiss, alias Mexican Joe Juniper.

Robbery & Murder

At just after ten o'clock on the evening of 4 February, Howard Pettybone, ensconced in a pleasant room in the boarding house of Lowell and Martha Seaborne, was preparing to retire. A knock came at his door, he opened it, and was staring into the barrel of a sawed-off carbine.

"Say nothing and back up. Sit down on your bed and listen."

Judge Pettybone understood the wisdom of discretion in its relationship to valor. He complied. "I want you to pen an order to the marshal. You will order him to provide a closed carriage for you at six o'clock tomorrow morning, down front. You will also order that the prisoner Juniper be shackled and transported in that carriage, with you, to court. Tell the marshal to provide a deputy for escort. Explain that the purpose of your order is one of assuring the security of the prisoner. Order him to stage a phony transport of Juniper to the court at about seven o'clock.''

Preacher walked to a writing desk in the corner, pulled out the chair, stepped back and motioned for the judge to move to it.

"You're making a very serious mistake, young man."

"That may be, your honor. Now don't you make one." If Judge Pettybone was anything, he was an excellent judge of men's attitudes. He judged that this tall, brooding man would, in fact, shoot him if he did not do as he was told.

When the order was written and signed, Preacher told Pettybone to call up the landlord and ask that his son deliver the message. Again, the judge complied. After the boy left the room and the landlord had returned to his own quarters downstairs, Judge Pettybone turned again to face his intruder.

"The marshal may very well be knocking at this door inside of fifteen minutes. That order I wrote is most unusual."

"I took the precaution of sending a boy to the marshal's office about half an hour before I came here, judge. The lad told him to expect a hand written, court order from you which would require no reply and the highest degree of discretion."

The judge sighed and sat down. He stared at the floor for several seconds, then he looked up.

"It's a clever ruse sir, I'll give you that." The judge pointed his finger at Preacher, "But you won't get away with it. Frankly, I'll be surprised if you and your cronies even get out of Cheyenne."

"Why don't you impose upon your landlord once more, judge. Ask them to provide you a pot of coffee —tell him you've a lot of preparation to do for court and that you'll be up late and do not wish to be disturbed." The judge looked puzzled. "It's going to be a long night," Preacher said.

The bounty hunter had slept almost all day long. He was refreshed, quick of wit and sharp of mind. He'd have no trouble staying awake. Though tired, Judge Pettybone's experience had roused new vitality within him as well.

Most of an hour was spent in silence. Furnished with coffee, the two men drank and stared at one another. It was Judge Pettybone who finally broke the silence.

"I can recall most of the men I've faced in my court room. I don't believe you're one of them, but you ring familiar to me, young man."

"I haven't been in your courtroom, judge."

"Your name?" The judge smiled. "If you win it won't make any difference. If not, I'll find it out anyway."

"Preacher." The judge looked thoughtful and then Preacher saw the expression lighten.

"A bounty hunter and an army scout." The judge pointed his finger again. "By Godfrey . . . you're not here to rescue Juniper from the gallows!"

"And I'm not here to collect the bounty that was on his head."

"You're here for those who would free him." Preacher nodded. "Who? Where are they?"

"They're near," Preacher said, "that's all I'm sure about. Who? I only know two, they're all I'm interested in. Brock Sturgis and Harry Griswold."

"You're still breaking the law this way."

"Your law, yes."

"There is only one law."

"No judge, there's Preacher's law. I'm enforcing it."

It didn't take too much effort on the marshal's part to let the word get out about Juniper's transfer from the jail to the courthouse. By midnight, Sturgis and the others knew about the seven o'clock time. Jack Henry had simply let the word filter into Cheyenne's saloons. Sturgis had kept the four cowpokes—none of them with wanted posters on them—in Cheyenne.

On schedule, deputy city marshal Isham King arrived at the Seaborn's boarding house. He acted both as a security guard and driver. Mexican Joe Juniper was shackled with both leg and wrist irons and sat inside the coach. King walked to the door of the house and, a moment later, was ushered upstairs at the invitation of Judge Pettybone.

Preacher put the butt of the mare's leg over the back of the deputy's head. He ordered the judge to bind the man to the bed, checked the ropes, slipped King's badge into his pocket, and he and the judge departed.

Preacher and Judge Pettybone climbed into the driver's seat. Preacher motioned for the judge to take the reins.

"Where to, gunfighter?"

"The courthouse," Preacher replied. The judge expressed surprise. Preacher gestured behind them with his thumb. "Joe Juniper is guilty as hell. Hang him, judge. If you don't, I'll be back."

The carriage moved forward. Judge Pettybone

said, "You may have ordered the marshal and his men to their deaths—some of them anyway."

"I took action two days ago, Judge. I let the word out about a phony transfer and that the real transfer would be done with a hay wagon from the livery stable at seven o'clock. I'm confident Sturgis and his cronies already knew everything but the time. Your marshal no doubt handled that last night."

"Don't be a damned fool, Preacher. I've no use for you, or men like you, but you can't ride in there alone."

"You just make certain Juniper gets the full measure of *your* law." At the rear entrance to the courthouse, the judge was surprised to find a young man waiting with Preacher's horse. Preacher paid the boy, mounted up, eyed the judge and flicked the brim of his hat as he rode away.

Once he was out of sight, Preacher dug his spurs into the mare's flanks and rode toward the Cheyenne stock pens. He'd lied to Judge Pettybone about the livery stable. He'd been certain the judge would do his best to foil Preacher's plans. He was right.

Even as he rode toward his destination, a frustrated Marshal, Jack Henry Upton, was wondering why he and his men hadn't been jumped. It was five minutes past seven and they were less than a block from the courthouse. He learned the reason a moment later.

Judge Pettybone, eliciting aid from three office workers in the courthouse, moved Joe Juniper into a holding cell. The judge then hastily scrawled a note to the marshal about the entire ruse and sent one of the office workers to deliver it. It included instructions for the marshal to ride, at once, to the livery barn!

# TRAIL OF DEATH

Brock Sturgis was fully convinced that he'd gotten accurate inside information. Everything he'd heard two days earlier had been confirmed. A phony transfer, a different time schedule. He believed he knew the truth. Joe Juniper would be at the Cheynne stock pens at 7:15. So as to avoid attracting too much attention, the marshal would have assigned only two deputies to guard him. So informed, Sturgis and Harry Griswold opted to ride in exactly at the appointed time, hard, fast, and shooting.

By ten minutes after seven, the man in black from Tennesse was hidden behind the auctioneer's platform, mare's leg at the ready. He'd pulled a two wheeled hay-hauler into position at one end of the auction arena, draped his hat over one corner of it to appear as though a man were standing near it, and then waited.

Brock Sturgis had not lived so long by being careless. He held up his hand when the stock pens came into view.

"Griswold, take two o' the men around the far end. Ride through shootin'. I'll send the other boys in on foot while you're gettin' in position. Make sure that marshal ain't up to somthin'. Me'n Laredo will cover this side. Anybody gets out, we'll be waitin'. Griswold nodded, motioned to two of the cowpokes, and the trio rode wide to the north. Preacher watched and waited.

The first of the gang to come under Preacher's guns were the two men on foot. He knew why they were there. He knew they saw his hat. He knew what they thought. A minute later, he heard the horses which signalled the arrival of Griswold.

Having received no signal of trouble, Griswold and his two saddle companions charged into the arena. Griswold died first, a heavy calibre slug tearing away half his chest. Three of the four remaining men went to their deaths just behind him. The fourth man, screaming "Ambush!" ran from the arena in panic.

Preacher let him go, dropped from his hiding place, mounted up and rode, retracing the route Griswold had taken coming in. In effect, he'd flanked Sturgis. Preacher didn't know about the gunny named Laredo.

"Goddam," Sturgis screamed when he heard the cowpoke's yell, "let's ride." He and Laredo both turned their horses. They had gone only forty or fifty yards when Preacher rode into view. The big bounty hunter reined in his mount, climbed down, took off his heavy coat, reloaded the mare's leg and walked toward the duo.

"That sonuvabitch is crazy," Sturgis said. Behind them, the men could hear the galloping of another horse fading. The cowpoke had deserted them. Laredo looked back toward the arena. Everything was quiet. He frowned and turned back.

"I think he's by himself," Laredo said. He looked at Brock Sturgis.

"It's that fuckin' bounty hunter—the Widow Maker." Laredo's eyes got bright. His mouth twisted into a smile. "J.D. Preacher's been lookin' for you?"

"I thought he was dead."

Laredo stepped down. "I'll take 'im, Sturgis, an' cancel your debt to me." Laredo removed his own heavy coat as he turned to face Preacher.

"Sturgis," Preacher shouted.

"Yeah," came the reply.

Preacher, until then, hadn't been certain which of

the men he wanted. Now he was. He fired. Brock Sturgis' eyes bugged out, rolled back in his head, he leaned forward and then slipped sideways from his horse. The bullet caught him in the stomach, passed through his vitals, severed his spine at the base and exited. He was dead before he hit the ground. Preacher dropped the mare's leg.

It had all happened so fast, Laredo hadn't time to react. Now, he realized that Sturgis was dead and the big bounty hunter would face him—one on one.

"It's up to you," Preacher said, "if you want to ride away from this. I got who I came for."

Laredo grinned. "You don't know me, do ya bounty man?"

Preacher didn't answer. "Name's Laredo. That mean anythin'?" Laredo was proud of what little reputation he enjoyed. He'd swelled it to proportions which it did not merit however. He felt angry that this gun fighter of so much legend and fancy did not even deign to respond. Preacher still didn't say anything. "You think all this," Laredo said, gesturing behind him and then down at Sturgis, "scares me off'n you?"

Preacher was conscious only of the time. He couldn't tarry too much longer in or around Cheyenne. By now, the marshal would no doubt know everything. Someone, even as distant as they were from town, would have surely heard the shots. Particularly, the deep roar of the mare's leg. Preacher had already said to the pink-faced Laredo all he'd planned to say.

"Now," Laredo shouted. The distance was some fifty to sixty feet. Laredo's draw was honed to a fine edge. Fast, smooth, and late! He was better than most Preacher had faced. He got off a shot. It grazed the edge of the sole of Preacher's left boot. Preacher drew from his vest holster and put his shot, dead center, in Laredo's chest. Ten minutes later, Preacher was riding north.

# 15

The country seemed as dead and desolate as Preacher's soul. He rode north, crossing Chugwater creek and the Laramie River. He rode in the snow, the biting cold and the winds which whipped down from the Big Horn range, the rain and the sleet. He felt nothing, no warmth of spirit, no icy hatred, no anticipation of the future, no regret of the past.

He reached the North Platte River. He found the skeletal remains of an Indian encampment—Crow he believed—and he used it. He remained there through much of March. Finding food for one man was little problem. It was winter so he knew there would be no intruders. There were none.

On the 22nd day of April, Preacher rode through the gates of Fort Fetterman. It was a few miles northwest of the settlement of Douglas, Wyoming territory. He paused in Douglas just long enough to resupply himself. Douglas had no law and the army had no dodger on him. He did take note of the considerable activity at Fetterman. Far more than the usual, he reckoned. Few of the troopers paid him any mind. He dismounted at the Fort's headquarters building.

"Sergeant," Preacher said, as he entered, "is the General in his office?" The sergeant looked up. He saw a man with dark circles under his eyes and a thick, heavy beard.

"He is, sir. But he is in conference."

"Tell him Preacher is here—J.D. Preacher."

The sergeant's jaw dropped. He started to reply but, instead, just got up and walked to the office door. He opened it, stuck his head inside and said, "General sir, the scout . . . J. D. Preacher is here to see you." Preacher heard the gravelly voice respond.

"Send him the hell in here." The voice belonged to the man the Indians called old Three Stars, General George Crook. Preacher entered, Crook didn't stand. He just looked and said, "You look like hell."

"You need a dispatch rider?"

"No." Crook motioned for Preacher to sit. The two other officers present weren't even introduced. Both were young and their uniforms had a West Point crispness about them. Their faces were free of even a hint of whiskers. Crook shooed them out with a wave of his hand. When the door closed, Crook said, "I need another scout."

"I'm not interested in scouting," Preacher said.

"I don't give a damn if you're interested or not." Crook opened a drawer on his desk, removed a wanted poster and handed it to Preacher. He read. The reward now being offered by Wells-Fargo was $2,500. Since the stage and express company had been under army contract, they had asked the army to take an active role in apprehending both those who had perpetrated the payroll robbery and the man who had murdered their station agent in Pierre.

"You turned lawman have you, General," Preacher asked, tossing the dodger back onto the desk.

"No. Army doesn't send men out looking, but you walk in here and I can arrest and detain you for civil authorities."

"And you'd do that?"

"Not if you'll scout for me."

"That legal?"

"I doubt it, but I don't give a damn. I need information a hell of a lot more than I need another line in my record that states I assisted in your apprehension."

"Where are the scouts you had?"

"I've still got them Preacher, and they're all in the field. Frank Grouard is my chief."

"He's a good man."

"Good as any, but he can still only be in one place at a time. I've got to know what we're up against."

"I read something couple of months back, a big campaign."

"The biggest," Crook said. He held out a cigar. Preacher declined. Crook bit the end off of one for himself and then lit it. "Whiskey?"

"You got Teton Jack?" Crook grinned and shook his head.

"You're the most particular son of a bitch I've ever run across. You could be dyin' of thirst and I swear, you'd die before you drank anything else." Crook got to his feet. "Well, as a matter of fact bounty hunter, I do." He fetched it, poured them each a short drink and then added, "and I don't intend that you drink it all up. Too hard to come by."

"Don't blame you General, and thanks, I'm grateful."

"You'd better be, grateful enough to go to work for me."

"Fill me in," Preacher said.

Only a month before, Crook explained, he had led a column of troopers north along the Bozeman trail. Up along the south fork of the Powder river, Crook's troopers encountered a Sioux encampment. Grouard was certain that Crazy Horse—the warrior leader, already a legend—was there encamped. Crook attacked.

Grouard made two mistakes. First, because he recognized markings of Chief He-Dog, he assumed Crazy Horse's presence. He was wrong. Second, he under-estimated the size of the camp. He counted the tipis but he did not allow that it was merely a base for the skinning of buffalo brought in from the hunt.

Crook told Preacher that he attacked the camp and exacted a victory very much similar to Custer's triumph, as Crook called it, at the Washita. Warriors were nearby and they retaliated. While Crook claimed a victory because the Indians had fled, the Sioux had, in fact, recaptured their pony herds and inflicted a serious casualty count on the retreating troopers.

"Seems a little early in the season for a buffalo hunt that big," Preacher observed.

"Unless there's more Indians gathered in one spot than at any other time in history."

Preacher considered the wily old General. Few men knew Indians better. Crook had fought in nearly every Indian campaign of any size on the frontier. "That what you think?"

"It is. We know," Crook said, moving to the wall map, "that most of the young warriors of the various Sioux tribes have already fled the reservations. Thing is, so have the Cheyenne, and I don't know how many others. The only Indians left to scout for me are a few Crows and Shoshonis."

"What's the general campaign plan?"

Crook poked at the map with his finger. "General Terry is in overall command. He'll move out of Fort Lincoln. General Gibbon will ride out of Fort Yates—Montana Territory. I'm to move north out of here."

"Three pronged attack, either box them in and force them west, or . . ."

"Or wipe them out in a single action."

"Seems solid." Preacher finished his drink. "You don't sound too enthusiastic."

"I'm not, Preacher. Too many things to ponder. Too much politics." Preacher frowned. "Custer! He's still in trouble. Hell, the little peacock strutted back to Fort Lincoln early this month. A week later, Grant ordered him placed under arrest for leaving Washington without permission. Ordered him brought back, under guard."

"Did he go?"

"Hell yes, he had no choice . . . but not without screaming. Terry wants him. Wants him bad."

"The Seventh?"

"Uh huh. Between Terry's foot soldiers, Custer's cavalry, my force here and Gibbon, we could handle almost anything."

"If you knew just what you were really facing."

"That, yes, and who will be commanding just what forces, and exactly how many hostiles are out there. And most important, where the hell they are!"

"Any ideas about that, general?"

Crook poked at the map again. Preacher followed the movement of Crook's finger. "Anywhere from here, in their sacred ground, west to the Big Horn mountains, southwest clear over to the rockies, or," he said, jabbing at the map, "up here in Montana territory."

"How long have you," Preacher smiled, "how long have *we* got to find out, General?"

Crook slapped Preacher on the shoulder. He smiled and pointed at the Teton Jack bottle, "One more, for that last question, Preacher." Preacher nodded. Crook poured. Both drank. "About two weeks, give or take ten days." Preacher looked surprised. "Yeah . . . I don't like it either. I tried to tell those stubborn bastards to find the leaders and hit—hard—in the winter. Hell, my men can fight a winter campaign. If we'd found Crazy Horse and Gall and Sitting Bull we wouldn't need this summer excursion."

"Give me today and tonight," Preacher said. "I'll ride out tomorrow. Where's Frank?"

"Grouard and three Shoshonis are riding into the Wind River country. I've got four Crow scouts checking the Big Horns. I'd hoped you'd ride into the Black Hills."

"The sacred ground? No need," Preacher said. "They won't go back in there, except a few renegades. It's been violated. They can only purge it with the blood of white men. A lot of blood."

"You know, by God, I think you're right." Crook chuckled.

"I read where Custer was givin' 'em hell, Grant mostly, about how the agents were cheatin' the Indians and how they'd turned his trail into the Paha Sapa to a road of thieves." Preacher turned at the words, and smiled. Custer had quoted him.

"I hope General Terry is able to get Custer back in time for the fight."

# TRAIL OF DEATH

"I do, too," Crook said, and then added, "as long as the little banty isn't in overall command."

"You don't think Custer is a good leader, General?"

Crook smiled. "Damn fine leader. Men will follow him most anywhere. He's just too brash to be a good commander. There's a difference, Preacher."

"Yes General, I agree."

Preacher quit Fort Fetterman the following morning. Trailing a pack horse with him, the Tennessean, barely more than six weeks past his thirtieth birthday, rode northwest. By early in May he was tracking numerous signs along the Yellowstone River. He continued his journey until he reached the landmark known as Pompey's Pillar. He'd been gone from Fetterman near 3 weeks. Numerous times, he'd seen both hunting and war parties of Indians. He'd been chased several times and forced to fight on two occasions. He knew he was very near to a main encampment, but he hadn't seen it. He didn't know where to look next and he was certain that Crook would already be moving north before he got back to Fetterman.

Preacher rode southeast from Pompey's Pillar. His destination was the next landmark he'd need to guide him to the east range of the Big Horns. Thereafter, he felt certain he would, at some point, encounter large numbers of Indians, or northern bound troops. On May 28th, Preacher reached the confluence of the Bighorn and Little Bighorn Rivers.

He was grateful for the changing season. While it turned quite cool at night, there was now the promise of summer in the heat of the midday sun. It was nearing dusk when he found what he considered a suitable campsite. He set about to spend the night. He secured his mounts, stowed his pack gear, broke open what he would need for cooking and then walked to a nearby rise to gather firewood.

The horizon to the south, not too distant because of the rolling, hilly landscape, was nearly obliterated by smoke. There was so much of it, Preacher concluded that he was witnessing either a massive prairie fire, or the result of a lightning strike in the Big Horn mountains.

He ate. The wind had shifted to the south so it would be warmer that night. He sat up and sniffed the air. Wood burning! Then, something else aroused his sense of smell. Meat cooking! Preacher carefully covered the most obvious signs of his camp. He moved his pack horse still further into the stand of trees, saddled the mare, checked his weapons and started south along the river. It was hard going, and after only some five odd miles, it was dark.

Preacher didn't hear the Indians. His mare did. By then, Preacher was on the ground and the warrior was about to bash in his skull. Preacher grabbed the brave's wrist. He could feel the ripple of his own muscles, every fibre straining against the power of the warrior. Suddenly, Preacher stopped pushing and pulled, hard.

The Indian, surprised by the sudden change, lost the initiative, and his war club. Preacher's free hand, his left, now struck out, knocking the warrior to one side. Preacher's speed and his Bowie knife did the rest. Just behind him he heard the rustle of brush, someone walking. He got to his feet and turned. There were three of them. Two charged at him. Preacher used his skill and killed all three with single shots. He reloaded and realized the mare had taken off.

# TRAIL OF DEATH

Preacher walked south along the river. Now, he used caution and kept ever alert. The braves he'd gunned were Cheyenne but the one who'd jumped him was Sioux. Hunkpapa Sioux. He stopped and crouched. He heard a noise so he moved carefully. He peered into the darkness. The mare was grazing peacefully, oblivious to what lay just beyond. A red glow danced on the crest of a ridge.

He reached his mount and led her to the hillock. What he saw below took even his breath away. Stretched for miles along the river were tipis. Fires burned before each. He could see the silhouttes of the village's residents moving about. He was certain this was the encampment for which he'd been searching.

Preacher's capture here could prove fatal to many hundreds of men. All of the talk about Indians uniting under a single leader seemed now to have become a reality. Certainly, even by the most conservative estimate, this village was home to a minimum of 2,000 warriors. Preacher knew what he must do. His awe precluded his immediate departure.

After nearly ten minutes, Preacher turned the mare and started walking back north, back toward his own tiny camp. By his reckoning, it was some 12 miles away. He barely covered a quarter of that distance before he emerged from the trees along the river and saw no less than two score of warriors on a ridge ahead of him. They also saw him.

Preacher gambled. The stakes were high—his life. He spurred the mare and rode west, screaming Indians hard on his trail. The mare was sure-footed but she lacked the speed his big stallion, Cap'n, had afforded him. He stayed low—as low as his huge frame would allow. Bullets came increasingly close to him and he knew that the Indians would ultimately tire of the chase and kill his horse.

He reached a deep coulee, rode along its edge, hell bent, for another mile and then, both mare's leg and Winchester under his arm, he slipped from the saddle. The mare raced on. The warriors raced by. None saw him. Preacher knew he'd seen the last of his mare.

# 16

Jim Hickok scarcely looked up when the man across the table from him got to his feet. After all, Hickok had taken more than $200 from him. A moment later, the chair moved again. Hickok was still engrossed in his current hand but the man's voice brought a quick reaction.

"I'll sit in an' see if'n we kin catch this tin horn cheatin'." Hickok's eyes flashed up and seemed to grow darker. Then, he found himself staring into the face of Lonesome Charley Reynolds.

"If I was cheatin' Charley," Jim Hickok said, grinning, "It'd take a damn better man than you to catch me." Hickok glanced around the table, smiled, looked at his chips and threw in a white one.

" 'Nother hundred," he said. There were no takers. "I'll be quittin' you gents for a time. Got a pard to visit.' "

"You always quit winning?" Hickok glanced at the newest man among them. The man was spoiling for trouble. Jim Hickok was tired of trouble.

"Wished I could say that, but it don't happen. Give you a chance at me a little later."

"I won't be here late," the man said.

Charley Reynolds leaned over the table. He was whispering, but it was somewhat a sham. Anyone within twenty feet could hear him clearly.

"No sir, you sure 'nuff won't if'n you persist in rilin' this gent. He's Wild Bill Hickok." The man studied Charley's face, realized he was serious, wiped his mouth, folded his hand, got up and walked out.

At the bar, Charley Reynolds wasted no time. "Jim, I need ya ridin' with me."

"No more scoutin'," Hickok said. "I got hitched up, down Kansas way. Come up here to do a little money makin.' "

"In this damn gulch?"

"Not a gulch anymore," Hickok said, grinning. "Goddam town now. Even got a name."

"What's that?"

"Deadwood they call it. Me'n Colorado Charlie got a spot outside."

"You ain't no prospector, Jim. Never was."

"How'd you find me?" Jim asked suspiciously and then added, "an' how's come you weren't surprised about me gettin' hitched. Or didn't you believe it?"

"I believed it," Lonesome Charley answered. "I read about it. Read about you riding north too, up here to the gulch."

"Damn kid. What's his name?"

"Nate Breed."

"Yeah. After Preacher man shot me up down in Pierre, that kid hasn't stopped doggin' me."

"That's because the story has it that he's the only

one what ever put a bullet in ya, an' you kil't him fer his trouble."

"I didn't, Charley."

"I know that Hickok, an' I know he prob'ly could o' kil't you."

Hickok grinned. "No prob'ly about it. By my reckonin' he'd put one between my eyes next time."

"He really beat you?"

"He shot me, didn't he?"

"Did he beat you Jim? Hell, you shot him too. Placed your shot same as him."

"Draw, I reckon." Jim took a drink of whiskey and lit a cheroot.

"Heard anythin' bout Preacher?"

"Stories. Cheyenne. Heard he got them he was lookin' for."

"They git him?"

"Nope. Rode out an' disappeared. He'll show up again. He always does."

"Jim, I need you. Custer needs you. He's back, commandin' the Seventh. We're gettin' ready to ride. Custer will be under Terry, but you know the Gen'rul."

"Yeah," Jim Hickok said, his face suddenly turning serious, "yeah, I do. That's what bothers me, Charley." Jim Hickok had been leaning on the bar with his elbows. Now, he straightened to his full height. "If what I been hearin' is factual pard, this is one to walk away from." Charley Reynolds frowned. "Bad medicine. Crows are ridin' south, way south. Talk is Sittin' Bull an' Crazy Horse, Gall an' Two Moon have put together a confederation."

"You believe that, Jim? You think anybody could put the Hunkpapas, Minneconjous, Sans-Arc, Oglala all together, an' then toss in some Blackfeet and Cheyenne just fer good measure?" Charley grinned.

Hickok didn't. "Stay out o' this one, Charley. Tell Custer to ride slow . . . look ever'where he's never looked before, an' don't move 'til he's sure that ever'thing he's seein' is ever'thing there is."

"You *do* believe it."

"I do, Charley. When we rode into this country," Hickok said, pointing to the floor, "to the Paha Sapa, well," he frowned, "the Preacher man said it best."

"How's that?"

"He said we raped the Indian's Virgin Mary. They don't seem too likely to forget that." Now, Hickok smiled, ever so slightly. "Besides, I told you, I got hitched."

"I'll be damned. The frontier'll go all to hell now for sure. Bunch o' little Wild Bill's on the loose." Charley laughed. So did Jim Hickok. They drank together, wondering if it would be the last time. The next morning, May 29, 1876, Lonesome Charley Reynolds rode out of Deadwood gulch, east, toward Fort Lincoln, Bismarck, Dakota territory.

Lonesome Charley Reynolds had been on a scouting foray out of the fort since the end of April. Like all the scouts, Charley had not ridden quite far enough. Those from the south didn't ride far enough north. Those, like Charley, riding from the east didn't venture west far enough.

Charley knew the country better than most men. He'd hoped to elicit aid from a man who knew the Indians. Few were superior to Jim Hickok in that regard. Now, disappointed in his entire trip, Charley would ride back and join the Seventh to ride into uncertainty.

In fact, Charley Reynolds didn't reach Fort Lincoln. Much had happened since he rode out of it.

# TRAIL OF DEATH

General Terry's pleas on behalf of Custer had borne fruit. Terry, with the help of General W.T. Sherman, and a score of Democratic politicians who often dreamed of a Custer Presidential campaign, wrested victory from a stubborn Ulysses Grant.

Grant was caught up in a number of scandals, and while he was personally innocent of most of the serious wrong-doings, his failure to act on those about which he was aware threatened to boil him in his own stew. Reluctantly, he agreed to return command of the 7th Cavalry to Custer, but only under the command of General Terry.

Custer had to hurry and he did. He arrived at Fort Lincoln on May 10. One week later, to the strains of "The Girl I Left Behind Me," the Seventh rode out. Libby Custer rode with her husband to the regiment's first camp site, about ten miles from the fort itself.

That evening Libby, Autie, Custer's two younger brothers, Tom and Boston, his teen-aged nephew, Autie Reed, and his brother-in-law, Lieutenant James Calhoun, had an unofficial celebration. This, they all believed, would be Pahaska's last campaign against the red man. His next one would be against the Republicans.

Lonesome Charley Reynolds joined the Seventh as they forded the Little Missouri River near the Dakota-Montana territorial boundary. Once across, mid-afternoon on the 3rd day of June, Custer called a halt. Charley, Bloody Knife and Custer met with Terry.

"Reynolds," Terry began, "the Indian scouts, both the Crow and the Arikara, tell me we are riding into the day of our last sun. Still, not a damned one of them can tell me where the Sioux are camped. Can you?"

"West," Charley said, pointing and moving his hand back and forth in an arc, "farther than we've been, ever."

"Suggestions, gentlemen?"

"Two," Custer said, without hesitation. "First we should dispatch a rider, probably one of the Crow scouts, south to intercept Crook. His own scouts may well have found what we're looking for." Custer looked up and smiled. "And he shouldn't get *all* the glory, should he?" Custer spoke in jest. Unfortunately, recent circumstances made it difficult for Terry to swallow the humor. He cast a scathing glance at Custer, whose face flushed. "Next sir, I believe that we should further divide this expedition."

"Custer," Terry said, his voice sharp and filled with disgust, "I asked for suggestions, not insanity. I have put much of my own career at stake to back you. Don't insult my intelligence by proposing that we further defy military logic."

Charley Reynolds winced. So did young Tom Custer. Both men knew how Autie reacted to such criticism. Both were proven wrong.

"You misunderstand me, General. Granted, the army is divided but the bulk of our strength is here. Your force sir, and the Seventh." Custer now warmed to his subject. "At the confluence of the Tongue and Yellowstone Rivers, I propose to cut south, thus locating the hostiles. It will place me equi-distant from both yourself and General Crook's forces moving up from the south. By then sir, we should know Crook's exact location. Also you will shortly be joined by General Gibbon. We can then coordinate an attack which will result in assuring that none of the hostiles will escape. After all," Custer said, smiling a cordial smile at his superior

# TRAIL OF DEATH

officer, "I doubt that you can argue that my Seventh Cavalry can move much quicker to positively locate the Indians than can your infantry."

General Terry studied the territorial map. He looked up, considering his young friend. Finally, he turned to Charley Reynolds. "What is your opinion?"

"We can't kill 'em, Gen'rul, 'till we find 'em. I'd a heap rather find them, than have them find us."

"Yes, of course. And we do need more information about General Crook." Terry sat down, crossing his legs and carefully considering the proposal. Finally, he shook his head in an affirmative gesture but he hastily added a condition. "I will take your plan under advisement, Custer. At the river junction we'll meet again. Gibbon will be there as well. So will the riverboat packet, *Far West*. We'll meet aboard her and discuss the matter again."

"And the riders south?"

"Send two. One Crow, one Arikara." Custer nodded.

Five days on foot, five days of hiding, not even risking a gunshot to kill game, J.D. Preacher reached the Rosebud River. He spent two more days fishing and resting. On June 5, Preacher finally found what he'd been counting on. Three Indians, mere boys, riding toward the great camp along the Little Bighorn. He knew that the Indians would have their own patrols out. He'd hoped to run into a small party—some number which he could, alone, handle.

"Hold," he shouted. He fired the mare's leg into the air, levered another shell into the chamber and levelled the barrel at the trio. Indeed he caught them by surprise but they were full of the fighting spirit of the Wakan Tanka. They charged. They died.

Again on horseback, Preacher carefully weighed his options. He knew that Terry, Custer and Gibbon were no doubt in the field by now. Was he closer to them than to Crook? He doubted it. He rode south, hard. He'd gone no more than half a day's ride from his starting point, rode over a ridge, and found himself facing more than a hundred Sioux and Cheyenne warriors. Some cut from the main body to give chase. Preacher rode east, then north.

In the forest and hills just east of the Tongue River, some fifty miles from where he'd started, Preacher lost his pursuers. He would lose more time. It was dark and the Indian pony was worn out. So was the bounty hunter. He camped.

Preacher slept fitfully that night. His memory was at work, turning his dreams into nightmares. He woke up a dozen times, certain that hostile Indians were upon him. He finally risked lighting his pipe. Then, he began to ponder the enormity of what he'd seen along the Little Bighorn. He had to find someone, soon. By morning, still physically drained, Preacher decided he could run no more risks. He would ride east, all the way to the Powder River, then south. He felt certain that none of the Indians would venture that far east. Granted, it would take him several days—ten or twelve likely, to make the circuit east, south and then back west to reach Crook, somewhere on the trail. Still, he would lose no more time having to run. He set out from the camp on the Tongue at daylight on the 6th day of June.

The Gods often play fateful games with their human pawns. Had Preacher but known it, he could have ridden due south that very morning, without

# TRAIL OF DEATH

interference from any man, white or red. As it was, Preacher was privy to the very information being sought by Generals Crook, Terry, Gibbon and Custer. While he was seeking to share it, they sought it with equal fervor.

On the morning of June 10, Generals Terry and Gibbon first met face-to-face. It was at the mouth of the Rosebud, where it branches off the Yellowstone. Gibbon had sent a dispatch rider to request the meeting. Custer, who wished to do some planning of his own, posed no objections when he was left in command of the entire Terry-Custer force. They camped at the mouth of the Tongue. On 12 June, Terry returned.

"We have learned nothing. Gibbon has made a thorough search of the Yellowstone country. There are no hostiles encamped to our west. You'll be pleased," Terry told Custer, "to learn that Gibbon is in full agreement with your plan. Have we heard from our Crow friends?"

"No sir, but we may be optimistic to expect their return so quickly. At all events," Custer said, smiling, "I took the liberty of detailing the campaign as we had discussed it earlier. I will take the Seventh to the south and then back to the west. Meantime . . ." Custer didn't finish. General Terry stopped him.

"Your audacity in the field may be worthy of more than you have been given, Lieutenant Colonel Custer, but *I* command this campaign and it is I, by God, who will issue the orders."

Custer, already treading on thin ice, was clearly surprised at Terry's attitude. Autie Custer had been certain he could wrap the old General around his little finger.

"General, I did not mean to assume authority."

"The hell you didn't, Custer. That is precisely what you meant to do." Terry pushed by Custer and walked around to where he could get an overview of the territorial map. He studied it a few moments, then he looked up and said, "You order Major Reno to take six companies south. I want a thorough reconnaisance of both the Tongue and the Powder River country."

"Sir, with respect, that is fool-hardy."

"It was *your* idea, Custer."

"No sir, it was not. Such a force would not be adequate if the hostiles were found, but it would alert them, perhaps frighten them off."

"Your objection is horse dung Custer, and you know it. Your objection is focused on the fact that, during those two or three days, Major Reno and not yourself will be in command." Custer's eyes dropped. It was the only reply Terry needed for confirmation of his observation.

Custer looked up. He would have to try another tact. "And your troops, General?"

"I'll leave in the morning. Gibbon and I will meet at the confluence of the Yellowstone and the Rosebud. If Major Reno finds nothing, then we can safely assume that the hostiles are either encamped along the Bighorn or farther south, perhaps in Wyoming territory. I should think we would know of Crook's whereabouts by then as well. Perhaps he will have already found the Indians."

"General, I cannot stress firmly enough my opposition to this plan. It weakens the Seventh and loses time. The Indians are well to the west, not in the Tongue or Powder country."

Custer was angry. In part, it was due to Terry's perception of why. He'd been right! Custer couldn't

# TRAIL OF DEATH

afford to lose the command to Major Marcus Reno, not even for a few days.

"The order is a compromise, Custer," Terry bellowed, "don't dispute me to the point where I am forced to relieve you. The issue is not up for discussion. When Reno returns, you may act on his report at your own discretion. That, sir, is the end of it."

J.D. Preacher had pushed too hard and too long. The little Indian pony simply gave out on him so he shot her. He was, once more, afoot. He was also running out of time. He started walking west. Indians or no, Preacher was also a gambler. He'd have to play the hand he'd been dealt, and he knew if it was a losing hand hundreds of men would die.

About mid-day on the 17th of June, Preacher topped a hill and fired a shot from the mare's leg. It got the desired results. The buzzards, feeding on human carrion, squawked, flapping their heavy wings and soared away from their feeding grounds. Preacher found the grisly remains of two men, both Indians—one a Crow, the other a Shoshoni.

Less than twenty miles to the west, General George Crook was leading his column of troops back to the south, licking the wounds inflicted upon him by the surprise attack of nearly 1,000 Sioux and Cheyenne warriors. They had been led into battle by Tashunka Witko, the Oglala Sioux, Crazy Horse. Crook had never made contact with the northern forces of General Terry. He knew now that he never would. His singie hope had been placed in the hands of J. D. Preacher. Crook was certain that Preacher was dead.

Major Reno, never one of Custer's favored officers, now incurred Custer's complete wrath. Reno, carrying out his orders from Terry to the letter, had made an even wider sweep than planned. He did not return to the Seventh's base camp at the mouth of the Tongue until June 20. After regaling Reno for more than an hour, he added the final insult and placed Captain Frederick Benteen in temporary command. Custer himself was faced with still more delay. He had a major war council to attend, with Gibbon and Terry.

Custer was so angered by Reno's actions that he barely paid attention to the legitimacy of the facts Reno did uncover. They were considerable. Definite proof of the movement, recently, of large numbers of hostiles to the west. Reno was convinced that the main Indian encampment was along the Bighorn River—the land the Indians called the Greasy Grass. Furious at Custer's attitude, Reno withdrew to his tent and found comfort in a whiskey bottle.

Custer, prior to leaving for the final council with Terry and Gibbon, took matters into his own hands. They were orders which he would not share with his superiors. He ordered Charley Reynolds and Bloody Knife to ride at least a day ahead of the regiment. The regiment itself was ordered to move out the following morning, march south along the Tongue for a day and then turn west. He would rejoin his regiment at a camp on the Rosebud. He set the date for the rendezvous on June 23rd.

On the evening of June 22, the official council completed, General Terry summoned Custer to his quarters. They were aboard the steamer, *Far West*.

"Custer," Terry began, almost the instant the two men were privately sequestered, "I want you to excercise your own discretion in the field." Custer's eyebrows raised. The earlier orders had been rather explicit. Terry waved off Custer's expression. "I know what I told you earlier. Mostly it was for the benefit of the others."

"Am I to understand, General, that I am free to act totally independent of this command?"

"Don't make more of it than I've said," Terry replied. "Our problem is not killing Indians. It's finding them, and making damned certain that the leaders do not escape."

"I'm not certain I understand you," Custer said, adding, "that is in regard to my role."

"Find them, Custer. You've got the best chance to do it. Get word to Crook—some contact or other, and then get word to me. They're down there, the Indians. A lot of them I think. Find them and keep them there until . . ." Terry paused, fumbled through some papers and found a calendar. He jabbed his finger onto the page. Custer looked— Monday, June 26, 1876. "Until then. By that day, I will be in position, myself and Gibbon."

"And Crook?"

"Crook too, if nothing has happened to him. If you've not heard, well, I believe the three of us can handle it."

"And if the Indians should try to flee?"

"That's a ponderable, Custer."

"Yes sir, but I'll be there . . . supposedly.

"If, as we believe, there is a large encampment, they won't be able to move out quickly."

"But if they try, sir?"

"I've said Custer, use your own best judgment. We'll coordinate a major attack on the 26th."

"Sir, will you write down my orders." Terry frowned. He considered the golden haired Custer the army's boy genius. The egomaniac. Terry thought Custer looked more soldierly than he'd ever seen him. He was in dress uniform, not the usual personal design which he wore. At Libby's request,

Custer had his golden locks shorn to collar length. Terry shrugged and wrote. Custer read.

22 June 1876
HQ Gen. A.H. Terry
Steamer Far West

Discretionary action may be required by Brvt. Gen. G.A. Custer in maintaining contact with the hostile forces when they have been located. A joint attack has been planned with the 7th Cavalry acting as an independent unit.

Signed,
A.H. Terry
Commanding

Custer was still not satisfied. He knew the situation and could still place several interpretations on Terry's orders. He considered pursuing the matter further but Terry's expression precluded it. That, and the fact that Custer believed he was holding a sure hand. He knew the Seventh was already two days ahead of where Terry believed them to be. Custer smiled, the two men shook hands. Terry wished him Godspeed and Custer left.

# 17

On the morning of June 24th, J. D. Preacher broke camp and began his southward trek again. He'd been walking less than an hour when his luck finally improved. He ran headlong into a 15 man patrol out of Fort Fetterman. It was under the command of Lieutenant L. W. Whitworth.

Preacher quickly told Whitworth what he knew. In turn, Preacher learned of the Sioux-Cheyenne attack which had driven General Crook from the field. Crook, he was told, was now regrouping for a forced march to the north.

"I doubt," Preacher said, "that there will be time for Crook to participate—if it's not already too late."

"Will you be returning to Fort Fetterman then?" Whitworth inquired.

"You're not riding on north?"

"No sir. Our orders were to make a two day ride out and back, to determine whether or not the hostiles might pursue our force or even plan an attack on the fort itself."

"Damn it, man. Terry, Gibbon, Custer and their forces have to be apprised of what happened down here. You're obligated," Preacher said, "to ride north and warn them."

"I'm obligated sir, to obey General Crook's orders." The lieutenant turned. "Off and on gentlemen, mount up." He turned back. "I repeat," he said, "will you be riding south with us sir?" Preacher brought the mare's leg up, fired one shot just over the lieutenant's head, levered another round in the chamber and lowered the barrel. The lieutenant's face paled.

"Dismount, lieutenant."

"I'll have you arrested and court martialled, sir."

"Dismount, now!" The lieutenant complied. Preacher turned the horse so that he might face the rest of the men. "One of you can double up with your commanding officer here," he said, "but any man who tries to be a hero will regret it." Preacher mounted. "Ride out, right now."

The big bounty hunter waited until the patrol was out of sight. Then, he turned north and rode like hell toward the Little Bighorn River. At top speed, he knew it would be well into Sunday, June 25th before he would see the Indian camp again.

On that same evening, Brigadier-General George Custer sat just outside his field tent sealing several dispatches. One was his version of Reno's scouting excursion and his account of the final war council aboard the *Far West*. It was to be forwarded to the New York *Herald* by way of the campaign's official reporter with the 7th Cavalry, Mark Kellogg of the Bismarck *Tribune*. Another would be sent to the

# TRAIL OF DEATH

Democratic National committee. In it, Custer stated that he would carefully consider a Presidential nomination. A third was a personal letter to Libby. In it, among other things even more intimate, Custer wrote,

> ... God, how I miss you! How I yearn for the sound of your voice. I am confident that a great victory here will assure our future. Still, if fate decrees another campaign, I can find no reason for you not to be along. You can stand the rigors and as I have so stated in the past, one bed should accommodate us both.

Custer sealed the last envelope and put it aside. He looked up to see his brother Boston approaching. He smiled. "Bos," Custer said, "you look like a damned minister. Why don't you find more comfortable dress?"

"A uniform perhaps?" Custer smiled. Boston was not in the army. Though he'd wanted to be, Custer had prevailed upon him to wait. He had plans for all the Custers—Autie Reed too—if he won the fame he expected to win.

"A broadcloth suit and a plug hat will suit you better," Custer said. "It's fitting for any Senator, or Congressman."

"You seem comfortable enough." Boston eyed the field dress his famous brother always wore. The boy was deeply impressed with his older brothers, and almost envious of Autie Custer's dashing appearance. The Seventh's commander now wore his heavy field trousers, a red shirt, and the white buckskin coat which he so cherished.

"Have you seen Tom?"

"No, but he was quite concerned earlier about the babbling of some of the scouts."

"Hmmm . . . which ones," Custer inquired, "the Crows or the Arikaras?"

"The Arikaras."

"Damned cowards." A horse, then another, both inbound, caught the brothers' attention. They were carrying Lonesome Charley Reynolds and Bloody Knife. Custer got to his feet. "Fetch Tom," he said. "Reno and Benteen as well." Boston Custer nodded and hurriedly walked away.

Gathered at Custer's tent, the oficers turned to Charley Reynolds. He at once deferred to the Crow scout, Bloody Knife.

"The Crow rode three more hours than I did," Charley said.

"Many Injun," Bloody Knife began, "all Injun together. Too many. Bad signs. They sleep in the Greasy Grass. You stay," Bloody Knife said, pointing to the ground beneath his feet, "wait for Three Stars Crook and the Walkaheap bluecoats of Terry." Bloody Knife had made his report. He stepped back, sat down Indian fashion and fell silent.

"Charley, this damn Crow going bad on me too?"

"Not Bloody Knife, Gen'rul. The Arikaras, yes, Most of 'em rode out before sun up accordin' to Curley. But Bloody Knife ain't lyin' to you, Gen'rul."

"You see the camp?"

"Not direct. Too damned many war parties out. But I'd reckon three, mebbe four thousand warriors."

Custer smiled. Among the group present, he was the only one who did. He considered the stern faces surrounding him. "This gentlemen, is what we rode out of Fort Lincoln to do."

"No t'ain't, Gen'rul," Charley Reynolds snapped. "We rid out to box them redskins in—you, Terry, Gibbon an' Crook. Seventh can't handle 'em alone."

"Don't you go sour on me, Charley. They spot us, they'll hightail it. You send Curley and Bloody Knife north, first thing tomorrow. They can move Terry and Gibbon a little faster. We'll move on to the Little Bighorn."

"Damn it," Charley said, "if'n they see us we'll have to fight. Now them wasn't the plans."

"I know the plans," Custer said. "They call for the Seventh to locate and hold the hostiles in place." He smiled. "If they attack us, I can hardly refuse to fight." Charley shifted the chew in his mouth, gave Custer a look of disgust and then spit. He slapped Bloody Knife on the shoulder and the big Crow got to his feet. Charley turned and motioned for the Indian to follow. Bloody Knife looked straight into Custer's eyes.

"Too many," he said. "You fight, you die." He raised his arm and swept it in an arc from left to right. "*All* die." He turned and followed Charley Reynolds.

"Autie," Tom said, "what are your orders?"

"Now then, that's what I like to hear. Reno! Benteen! Take a lesson from my little brother. This is the *Seventh*. I don't give a tinker's dam how many hostiles are camped out there."

Sunday, June 25, 1876, dawned clear and warm. By 11:30 it was hot—near 95 degrees. Swarms of flies pestered the horses when they were not moving at more than a trot. Custer, disgusted with the attitudes of the Indian scouts, sent the lot of them packing at mid-morning. As ordered, Bloody Knife rode north. Acting alone, Charley Reynolds rode ahead of the column and finally topped the last ridge between the Seventh and the valley of the Little Bighorn River. Even the grizzly old scout had not seen the likes of what met his eyes this day.

"Jehosophat!" Trailing north for what Charley reckoned was three or four miles was a string of tipis. Even at that distance, Charley could make our signs of various tribes. Sans Arc, Minneconjous, Blackfeet, Assisiboine, Cheyenne, Oglala and Hunkpapa. He could see movement in the camp. It puzzled him because it appeared to be routine. He'd seen no patrols, no scouting parties, no signs to indicate the Indians were expecting the arrival of troops. He turned and rode back to the column.

He met Custer just as the column had reached the spot where they had found a lone tipi. Custer and his brother had dismounted and were examining the find. Charlie Reynolds joined them.

"I've never seen anything like this," Custer said, pointing.

"I'll be damned," Charley said. Custer looked up. Riding over the ridge just behind them was Bloody Knife and General Gibbon's personal chief of scouts, Mitch Bouyer. Custer felt a twinge of fear. He'd waited too long. Gibbon and Terry were at the scene.

"General," Bouyer said, dismounting. He spoke to Custer but his eyes were on Charley Reynolds. Between them, the two men had been on the frontier for more than sixty years. Both knew what lay beyond the ridge.

"Terry and Gibbon," Custer said. The words were tentative. Bouyer shook his head.

"The General sent me south five days ago to find what I could find and report back. I ran into three war parties and was forced east. I decided my best bet was to find you. I met Bloody Knife 'bout an hour out."

Bloody Knife stepped forward. He slipped his knife from his sheath, raised it and threw it to the ground. It stuck. "I stay," he said, pointing to the sun. "It is a good day to die."

Mitch Bouyer was as highly a respected man on the frontier as Cody, Hickok, Reynolds—even Bridger or Carson. He shunned publicity and rarely went into a town much bigger than Bismarck. Now, he looked George Custer straight in the eye. "Sometime about mid day tomorrow, Gibbon and Terry will be here. Bloody Knife told me you still haven't located General Crook. If I were you, I'd ride back east, fifteen, maybe twenty miles and camp. Set up a defensive perimeter and wait."

"Wait!" Custer was miffed. The Democratic National Convention was about to begin. He'd already penned a dispatch which described a great victory and credited him with carrying the brunt of the action. He could easily re-write it if events so dictated. Wait? Never!

"You move against that village General, and you won't have a man left. It's too big. I've never seen one like it in thirty years."

"And," Custer said, shrugging, "you've never ridden with the Seventh cavalry. We'll hem them in," Custer said, smiling, "make sure they've got no place to slip out. Tomorrow—victory."

"General, if you move any closer to that village than you are right now, they'll take it as a move against them. They'll fight you! This tipi is the boundary—the line of challenge. In God's name General, don't do this."

Custer called a staff meeting. Without a word, he'd dismissed the best advice of his scouts. He ordered Major Reno and three companies to move down the river at the south end of the camp. That, he said, would seal off the southern escape route. He did want to make certain that there were no large war parties already outside the camp. He ordered Captain Benteen with three companies, to scout to the south and west. He took personal command of the remaining five companies and stated only that he would ride the ridge overlooking the encampment and determine that it was not preparing to move.

"General," Bouyer complained, "you're dividing an already inferior force sir."

"If Major Reno is faced with problems, myself or Benteen will be in a position to ride to his support. We are not divided sir, we are assuming an offensive posture."

Benteen reluctantly rode south. Mitch Bouyer rode with him. Major Reno, in company with the Crow scout Bloody Knife, moved down the ridge toward the Little Bighorn. Charley Reynolds, a knot in the pit of his stomach, rode with Custer and the Gray Horse company. They waved to one another. It was 12:15.

J.D. Preacher couldn't believe his eyes. He saw the guidon with the big "7" emblazoned upon it. He shouted. Captain F. W. Benteen called a halt.

"Great God," Benteen said, eyeing Preacher's mount, "You're riding with Crook. We've received the Lord's blessing." Preacher frowned. Benteen explained, quickly, what had occured during the morning hours.

Preacher said, "Captain Crook met the Sioux more than a week ago—south of here. He got whipped. He's back at Fetterman." Benteen's face paled. "We've got to get to Custer. Surely he won't

# TRAIL OF DEATH

ignore *this*." Benteen nodded and the column turned back north. It was 1:22.

Fred Benteen and J. D. Preacher were the first men to find Major Marcus Reno. He sat, almost in a fetal position, behind a breastworks atop a bluff. The din of the firing was almost deafening. Reno's men were being systematically destroyed as they allowed an orderly withdrawal to become a panicked rout.

"We've got to get to Custer. Where is he?" Reno said nothing. He only looked up, tears in his eyes. "Damn it Major, answer me," Preacher shouted. Benteen knelt beside him.

"I've positioned my men on the bluffs. We can hold here."

"I've lost half my command," Reno said. His voice was trembling, his hands shaking. "Half, Benteen . . . and Custer never returned to help me." Preacher turned on his heel. He started out. Reno spoke again. "Look," he said, "look at this blood. God, it's Bloody Knife's brains. He was right next to me."

Preacher dashed out, rounding up ten men and ten horses. They rode from the bluffs along the ridge Custer had taken. Less than half a mile along the spine of the ridge, they were confronted with a swarm of Indians—Preacher reckoned more than two hundred. They fought, fell back, got support from a contingent of Benteen's fresh troopers and held. They tried twice more to negotiate the ridge and failed in both attempts. It was near 2:30.

Reno, realizing that the position he'd taken up was tenable, regained some of his composure. He, Benteen and Preacher sat down about half an hour later. Reno told of what he had encountered in the valley. Benteen produced the message which trumpeter John Martin had toted from Custer. Preacher read it. In fact, it had been hastily scrawled by Custer's Adjutant, W.W. Cooke.

Benteen
   Big village. Be quick. Bring packs.
                                    W.W. Cooke

P.S. Bring packs.

The trio agreed that the only course of action open to them was defensive. Dig in, strengthen the breastworks, bring up additional ammunition from the pack train and ask for volunteers to move to the river and fetch water. The men, particularly those suffering wounds, were crying out for water. The heat was oppressive and the dust suffocating. The meeting broke up at 3:15.

Preacher and five other men negotiated the treacherous bluffs and reached the river. They filled canteens which were tied together with rope. Each man carried twenty five. Three of the men never reached the top of the bluff again. Preacher got back with fifty canteens of water. The attacks diminished and then stopped. It was 4:10.

J.D. Preacher rode across the field at just past noon on Monday, 26 June, 1876. His mind dislodged memories of the stories his father had related to him about the final day—March 6, 1836, at the Alamo. Preacher rode north, eight miles up the Bighorn River. There, he boarded the *Far West*. Behind him lay Tom and Boston Custer, Autie Reed, Mark Kellogg of the *Tribune*, Bloody Knife, Lonesome Charley Reynolds, 261 cavalry troopers who rode with Custer and Brevet General George Armstrong Custer.

Custer had believed his own words—perhaps he'd believed his own press. He was convinced that the Seventh cavalry could ride over the entire Sioux nation. To his enemies in that great camp, June 25, 1876 had been a *Ho-kay hey!* A good day to fight. A good day to die.

# 18

The *Far West* reached Bismarck on the afternoon of July 5. The earliest the Bismarck *Tribune* could publish its extra edition, the first printed account of the bloody battle, would be the next day. Preacher was grateful. He rode directly to Fort Lincoln, and by-passed reporting to the commanding officer. That duty fell to Captain Benteen. Preacher walked to Custer's quarters and knocked. Libby opened the door.

"Preacher! Oh my, this is a pleasant surprise!" She stepped aside, as Preacher entered. Libby Custer closed the door, Preacher turned and their eyes met. She sucked in a short breath, stepped back and steadied herself against a small corner table. "Which of them is it?" she asked. Preacher couldn't answer. He swallowed. "Tom? Boston?" Libby eyes grew large. Preacher's mind flashed back to his visit from Charley Reynolds and Hickok.

"All," he managed. Libby swayed. He started

# TRAIL OF DEATH

forward. She held up her hand and worked her way to Autie's favorite chair. She gripped its back hard.

"All of them?"

"Overwhelmed. Five companies." Libby moved around the chair and sat down. She smiled and nodded toward the love seat across from her. Preacher sat.

"When?"

"The twenty fifth of June."

"A Sunday. My Autie died on a Sunday. It was his favorite day—our day he called it. Oh Beau, oh Dear God, my poor Beau."

"Libby, I know what you're feeling."

She considered him, smiled and nodded. "Yes," she said, "you would." She stood up and smoothed her dress. "What companies?"

"C . . . E . . . F . . . I . . . and L."

"They—the wives, they'll need me now." Libby Custer stepped to where Preacher now stood. She stretched up on her toes and kissed his cheek.

"Libby, you should . . . well, rest." He thought the statement stupid. It was too late.

"Rest, Preacher? Did *you* rest?" He shook his head. He did understasnd. He walked with Libby Custer to the commanding officer's quarters. There, the women of Fort Lincoln were gathered. Preacher spoke once more to Libby Custer.

"Jim Hickok? Do you know . . ." she was already shaking her head.

"He didn't go. Charley Reynolds tried to hire him on. He was in the hills—the Black Hills. A mining camp."

"Deadwood Gulch?" She nodded. He gripped her hand, then, J.D. Preacher walked out of Fort Lincoln.

Preacher could barely believe his eyes. He'd ridden through this very gulch during the expedition in '74. Now it was a town. He couldn't help wondering where it had come from. It had the appearance of having always been there. He arrived in Deadwood in the early evening of July 28th. He had taken a rather circuitous route to get there. He'd gone to the south of it and rode back through the Paha Sapa. Indeed, Custer's golden road to glory was now a road of thieves. Still, the Indians had elicited from Custer a very dear price for his moment of glory.

Preacher had little trouble finding the likes of Jim Hickok. Wild Bill was playing poker in the casino of the Bella Union. He sat in a corner chair and when he spotted Preacher, his face broke into a wide grin.

"I'll be Goddamed," he bellowed and got to his feet. He whipped out one of his Colts, banged its butt against the table top and then shouted, "This here gent in the buryin' clothes is the only white man who ever put a bullet into Wild Bill Hickok. Gents, I heard tell he rode with old Yellow Hair over on the Big Horn, put the Griswold brothers in the ground an' blowed a hole in Brock Sturgis big enough to stick your fist into. Let's drink to muh friend Preacher, the Widda Maker."

Preacher didn't appreciate the publicity, but he couldn't help but smile. Half an hour later, he and Hickok sat in Hickok's camp tent with Colorado Charlie Utter.

"I tol' Lonesome Charley Reynolds to ride away from that fight, Preacher man."

"He wanted to, but you know Charley. He was hired so he rode."

"Helluva fight, wasn't it?"

"There'll never be another one like it, Jim,"

Preacher said.

"I read about it in the *Tribune*. You been back to Lincoln?"

"That's where I came from."

"Libby?"

"I don't know, Jim. She seemed fine. All she could think about were the other wives."

Hickok nodded and smiled. "That there is Libby Custer alright. She'll make it better'n most. Things won't seem right no more without Custer ridin' herd on the Sioux. Lord knows what the army'll do now."

"A blood bath I'd guess."

"Prob'ly. Well sir, I'll have no truk with it."

"No Jim, I won't either. The Bighorn was my last job for the United States army."

Hickok frowned, reached into his pocket and pulled out a dog-eared dodger. He unfolded it. "You've got real popular since Pierre." The reward was up to $5,000 on Preacher's head. "This scoutin' job won't hurt you none—if you can get Crook to write somethin' down. Him, an' Benteen an' Reno mebbe."

"Don't know, Jim. Seems to be they'll all be pretty busy for a spell. I figure those congressional buzzards back east will have a field day with this one."

"That they will," Charlie Utter said. "It's just as well ol' *Pahaska* got his out there. Hell, if Custer had survived, they'd have court-martialed him and prob'ly strung him up."

"Uh huh," Hickok agreed, "by his vitals."

"Well Preacher, what direction you ridin'?"

"I'm broke," Preacher said, "flat, Charlie. You've got no law here, so there's nobody to pay bounty."

"Hell, Preacher man, you can't walk into a lawman's office an' pick up bounty anyways. You got a price tag on your own hat."

"Yeah, that's another problem."

"An' as soon as Breed an' that damn Ned Buntline hear 'bout you still breathin' after ridin' with Custer, you'll be all over the front pages. Ever' damned bounty huntin' sonuvabitch west o' the big river will be lookin' for ya."

"Throw in with Jim and me," Colorado Charlie said. "We can grubstake you to enough poker 'til you get a poke o' your own. Besides, they's a few women ridin' into the gulch."

"And a few gunnies too, I'd guess."

"Them too Preacher man, but it'll be worse south o' here."

Preacher nodded. "You've got yourself a partner," he said.

Colorado Charlie worked the small claim that he and Hickok had staked out. It had netted little more than table stakes since they'd started working it but Jim Hickok's poker skills kept them in food and drink. Now, J. D. Preacher's skills were added to the collective pot.

On the evening of July 30, Preacher met Jim Hickok at the Bella Union casino. Preacher looked concerned.

"What's eatin' at you, bounty man?"

"Heard some talk about a fella who's gunnin' for you, Jim." Preacher frowned. "Did you ever kill a man name Phil Coe?"

"Sure did. Gamblin' man down in Abilene."

"That the time you gunned your own deputy?"

"The same," Hickok said, his face contorted with the memory. "Damn young fool come up on me from behind right during the shootout."

"Anyhow Jim, this gent says he'll get you. Somewhere, sometime."

# TRAIL OF DEATH

"Got a handle?"

"Jack McCall." Hickok laughed. "That funny is it?"

"It is with McCall. He's been doggin' my trail for two, three years now, by God. He's not worth a pinch o' cow dung. No gunman, just a windbag."

"He could hire somebody."

"McCall? Good Gawd. Jack McCall never had more'n the price of a drink in his poke once in twenty years." Hickok laughed again. "Now you go an' tell me that Johnny Hardin is gunnin' for me an' I'll do some deep considerin', but not Jack McCall." Preacher shrugged.

The two friends settled into a lengthy—and increasingly expensive poker game at the Bella Union. July 30 turned to August 1. About four o'clock in the morning, Hickok called a halt to the game so that the players could eat breakfast. They agreed to return to the table at seven o'clock that morning.

Hickok and Preacher ordered steak and eggs and then Hickok stepped out back to relieve himself. A moment later, three men entered the Bella Union. They all wore double rigs. Preacher, seated at a table near the rear door, was sipping coffee. He looked up. One of the men looked at him. He whispered to the other. The third man had approached the bar.

"I'm looking for a tall man dressed in black." He held out a dodger. The barkeep looked at it. He swallowed and his eyes darted toward the table at which Preacher was seated. Preacher was already alerted to trouble. He shoved his chair back and got to his feet.

"You the Widow Maker?" the man at the bar asked.

"I am," Preacher said.

The man smiled. He backed up and the trio spread further apart. The man spoke again. "I'm Anse Dobie," the man said. "The boy way over is my brother Will. In the middle there, that's Ely."

"You boys won't get rich killin' this gent," a voice said. It came from the rear of the building, behind Preacher. Jim Hickok stepped into view right beside the tall Tennessean. "Reward on him is only five thousand."

Anse Dobie picked up the dodger and held it in front of him. "Twice that, Mister Hickok." Dobie smiled. "They want your friend down Cheyenne way too. Real bad. Bonus if he comes in breathing."

"I won't," Preacher said.

"Suit yourself gun fighter, but don't figure your reputation will save your hide." Anse Dobie looked back at Hickok. "Or your friend's. I've heard stories, so have my brothers. That's where we've got you. We been workin' the southwest while you two been up here killin' redskins. Now we *know* what to look for. You don't."

"I've heard of you Dobie," Hickok said. Dobie smiled. "Heard o' your brothers, too." Preacher was somewhat confused by Hickok's dialogue, but not surprised. J. D. Preacher had determined that he would never be caught surprised again. It hurt too much, and it could prove fatal.

"What did you hear," Dobie asked, and then added, "Marshal Hickok?"

"I heard you were a bunch o' big-mouthed, back-shootin' blowhards." Anse Dobie reacted. He frowned.

"Who you want, Will?" Anse asked.

The man to the far right grinned. "Me an' Ely will take the Widow Maker, so's you can have Mister Hickok all to yourself."

# TRAIL OF DEATH

Just outside the Bella Union a crowd had gathered. Men were pressing their faces to the window trying to get a better view of the action. Little boys had slipped beneath the bat wing doors and secreted themselves beneath tables, behind chairs and almost anywhere else which afforded both safety and a view.

"You seem to let Hickok do all your talkin' for you. He shoot for you too?" Preacher didn't reply. "He piss for you, bounty hunter?" Preacher remained silent. "Hell, maybe Hickok even fucks your women for you." Anse Dobie laughed. "That's prob'ly how come they named you Preacher." Anse Dobie laughed again. Anse Dobie died laughing. Preacher's bullet struck him in the forehead. Anse had both guns in his hands but neither one was ever fired.

Will and Ely Dobie were not quite up to their brother—and nowhere near Jim Hickok. One of them did manage to blow a piece of the fringe off of Hickok's buckskin coat. Hickok's bullets entered the boys' hearts.

Very late that night, Hickok and Preacher returned to their camp. Colorado Charlie Utter was still awake and he'd heard about the gunplay.

"Keep a sharp eye from now on, Preacher man," Charlie Utter said. "Them boys were fair to middlin' gun hands, but they were just hired out." Preacher frowned. "You recollect that bounty man down Denver way Jim, name o' Miller Creek?"

"I do. Saw him drop two fellas at about seventy feet. Hit 'em both in the belly. Carried a short barreled forty four." Hickok looked at Preacher. "Heard of 'im?"

"It rings," Preacher said. "Never saw him that I know of."

"Stage driver told me he was down at Pierre not more'n a week back askin' about you. Same driver saw Creek and those three you put under a day or two later. Then the three rode out."

"Thanks Charlie, I'm grateful." Charlie nodded.

"I'm turnin' in," Hickok said. "I got an early mornin' game with Cap'n Massie. You want to sit in, Preacher?"

"Thanks Jim, but no. I've got enough of a stake to get myself a mount. Guess I'd better see if I can round one up."

Preacher found no suitable horse for himself until mid afternoon. When he did, he was more satisfied than he had been since he'd acquired Cap'n, the big stallion he rode for so long. This animal too was a stallion—all black save for four white stockings. Preacher couldn't think of an appropriate name so he decided to wait until evening and solicit the help of Jim Hickok and Colorado Charlie.

He'd purchased the animal from a newly arrived carpenter and his family. Preacher paid a slighty higher price than he'd wanted to, but his luck had been running good lately. He'd make up the difference at the poker table.

At a few minutes past four o'clock on the afternoon of August 2nd, Preacher reined up in front of the Bella Union. He noted the many passers-by who now stared at him. Until the gun play against the Dobie boys, J.D. Preacher had been somewhat a non-entity in Deadwood. A small group of men knew who he was only by virtue of Hickok's boisterous welcome. Most citizens had not known him and many did not even recognize Hickok. The shootout had changed all that.

Preacher entered the Bella Union. Two men sat at

# TRAIL OF DEATH

a corner table drinking beer and chatting. Neither looked up. At the bar, Preacher saw a tall, pleasant looking young man. Behind the bar stood Harry Young. He was the assistant manager and daytime barkeep at the establishment.

"Afternoon," Harry said, tentatively. Preacher merely nodded. He strode to the bar. "What'll it be," Harry asked.

"Nothing," Preacher replied. "I'm looking for Hickok."

"Haven't seen him."

The pleasant faced young man cleared his throat. Preacher turned and considered him. he was smiling. "Uh . . . he . . . he's in there," the young man said, pointing. He was indicating the archway which separated the Bella Union's casino from Nuthall and Mann's Number Ten saloon. "B'lieve he's playin' cards, Mister Preacher."

"I'm grateful," Preacher said. He started by the youth.

"Mister Preacher . . . uh . . . could . . . I mean . . . would you shake my hand?"

Preacher eyed the young man, looking for signs of a weapon. There were none. Preacher, a faint smile on his lips, shook the young man's hand.

"Muh name's Peter LeFlemme, and I'm mighty proud to make your acquaintance sir."

"Thanks again," Preacher said. He walked away and the youth, taking a deep breath, ordered another beer and moved nearer to the archway.

Jim Hickok sat at a small, square table which was located very near the center of the saloon. At the table with him were three men, two with whom Preacher was acquainted. Captain John Massie, a retired riverboat captain, sat immediately opposite Hickok. On Hickok's right was a sometimes gambler, shotgun rider and driver for the McClintock freight line, Con Stapleton. On his left sat one of the Number Ten's two owners, Carl Mann.

"Gents," Preacher said. They had just finished a hand and all of them looked up.

"Want you to meet Con Stapleton," Hickok said, pointing. He turned to Con. "This is J.D. Preacher."

"The bounty man they call Widow Maker?"

"The same." Stapleton got to his feet. He was a big man with a leathery look to him and he wore an eye patch on his left eye. He and Preacher shook hands but exchanged no dialogue.

"Buy you a drink, Preacher?" Carl Mann asked.

"No thanks."

"Get yourself a horse, Preacher man?"

"I did, Jim. Stallion—three and half, mebbe four. Fine mount, I think." Con Stapleton was dealing another hand. He looked up.

"Care to sit in?" Preacher shook his head.

"You riding back to camp?" Preacher inquired.

"An hour maybe, or a little more." Hickok grinned and pointed to his winnings. "Too good a streak to break."

"I'll drop back then. Got some possibles to pick up." The barkeep, Anse Tippie, approached the table.

"You gents ready for another round?" The men nodded. Anse looked at Preacher. "You drinkin'?"

"Later Anse, thanks."

Preacher strolled around behind Hickok. It was then he realized that Jim was sitting with his back to the open door. It struck him odd. Jim Hickok had lived by his hard, fast rule—"Keep your back to the wall."

"Must be a damned lucky seat," Preacher observed, "for you to expose your backside."

# TRAIL OF DEATH

Hickok looked up. "These gents wouldn't change with me. It's them what's livin' with lady luck." Preacher smiled and patted Hickok's shoulder. Hickok picked up his hand. Both he and Preacher eyed it. A pair of aces, a pair of eights and a nine of spades.

"Good luck, gents," Preacher said.

"See you shortly," Jim replied. Preacher waved at Anse Tippie and walked out of the Number Ten saloon. He paused and looked both ways, trying to recollect the direction of the Bighorn General Store. Determining that it was to his left, Preacher turned and started up the street. A third of a block later, a short, rotund man bumped into Preacher. The two danced the side-step for a moment, trying to pass one another. Preacher grinned. The short man didn't. He finally pushed his way by the bounty man and hurried away. Another half a block later, Preacher heard a gunshot. He stopped, tensed and turned.

Preacher heard some shouts. A moment later, a man could be seen backing out of a doorway. Once clear, he pointed a pistol back inside and fired again, then he turned and bolted away. Preacher recognized him as the man who had bumped into him only a minute or two earlier.

Suddenly, two more men appeared in the doorway. One of them was Anse Tippie. The man had come out of the Number Ten saloon. Preacher pushed two men aside, darted into the center of the street and ran toward the saloon. Anse Tippie was shouting.

"Stop that man. Stop him! He's killed Hickok." The man was running in the opposite direction. Several men now took up the chase. Preacher then saw the young man named Peter LaFlemme emerge from the Number Ten. By now, Preacher was within earshot.

"Get Doc Pierce. Cap'n Massie's hit." LaFlemme nodded and darted across the street.

Preacher reached the entrance to the Number Ten. Anse Tippie had just stepped back inside. Preacher walked in, stopped and looked at the table. Captain Massie was still in his chair. He was holding his left arm. Blood oozed from between his fingers.

Con Stapleton stood at the bar, his hands shaking as he tried to negotiate a shot glass from the bar up to his lips. Carl Mann was hunched over the body of Jim Hickok. He looked up.

"It was Jack McCall," he said. "Walked in, stepped behind Wild Bill, pulled out a pepper box and shouted 'Take that, damn you.'" Mann had tears in his eyes. "Goddam gun didn't even fire the first time." Preacher could see one of Jim Hickok's pistols was out, held loosely in his right hand. He'd still managed the draw before McCall's bullet struck him in the back of the head. It passed clear through Hickok's brain, exited the front of his skull and lodged in Captain Massie's arm. Jim Hickok died instantly.

Carl Mann straightened up as Doc E.T. Pierce entered the saloon. He was followed by Peter LaFlemme. Standing in the archway leading to the Bella Union was the barkeep, Harry Young. Preacher walked to the table as Doc Pierce, realizing he could do nothing for Hickok, began treating Captain Massie's arm. Preacher looked down and flipped over the hand of cards upon which reposed Jim Hickok's left hand. He'd thrown in the nine and drew the five of diamonds. He held the winning hand—Aces and Eights.

Preacher rode out to the camp and informed Charlie Utter of the tragedy. Colorado Charlie said nothing. He mounted up and rode into town to fetch Jim's body back. The next day, he and Preacher laid *Wild Bill* out in the tent. Both men were surprised by the number of Deadwood's citizens which showed up. Late the afternoon of August 3rd, they buried Jim. Colorado Charlie carved out a simple, wooden headboard.

**WILD BILL**
J.B. Hickok
killed by the assassin
Jack McCall
in
Deadwood Black Hills
August 2, 1876

Pard, we will meet again
in the happy hunting ground,
to part no more.

Good Bye
Colorado Charlie
C.H. Utter

# Epilogue

On the fifth day of August, 1876, J. D. Preacher rode away from Deadwood. He did so on the back of his black stallion, Prince. The name was Preacher's tribute to a gent who'd been both a Prince among men and a Prince of Pistoleers. He toted with him J.B. Hickok's dispatch case—a parting gift from Colorado Charlie Utter. It was the single item which had bound Hickok and Preacher together over the years.

Preacher rode south, through the Paha Sapa. It was scarred with the diggings of the white men who had violated its sanctity. He travelled along the very trail he'd helped to forge. It had become his personal thieves' road. It had taken from him Custer, Reynolds, Hickok, and Shannon MacKenzie.

Preacher remembered Jim Hickok's words. "I'm alone, but never lonely. Lonely hurts too much." Preacher remembered the only rule Hickok ever broke. "Keep your back to the wall." They had been James Butler Hickok's philosophies. Now, they were part of Preacher's Law.

# Make the Most of Your Leisure Time with
# LEISURE BOOKS

Please send me the following titles:

| Quantity | Book Number | Price |
|---|---|---|
| _____ | _____ | _____ |
| _____ | _____ | _____ |
| _____ | _____ | _____ |
| _____ | _____ | _____ |
| _____ | _____ | _____ |

If out of stock on any of the above titles, please send me the alternate title(s) listed below:

| | | |
|---|---|---|
| _____ | _____ | _____ |
| _____ | _____ | _____ |
| _____ | _____ | _____ |

Postage & Handling _____
Total Enclosed $ _____

☐ Please send me a free catalog.

NAME _____
(please print)

ADDRESS _____

CITY _____ STATE _____ ZIP _____

Please include $1.00 shipping and handling for the first book ordered and 25¢ for each book thereafter in the same order. All orders are shipped within approximately 4 weeks via postal service book rate. PAYMENT MUST ACCOMPANY ALL ORDERS.*

*Canadian orders must be paid in US dollars payable through a New York banking facility.

Mail coupon to: **Dorchester Publishing Co., Inc.
6 East 39 Street, Suite 900
New York, NY 10016
Att: ORDER DEPT.**